A Life Beyond the Mirror

Nicole Adams

Artwork by Phoebe Bruce

*To my loving Grandparents. Thank you for your unwavering support and
love and constant encouragement.
And to my Mother and Father, who taught me all that
they know and that anything is possible.*

Contents

Title Page	1
Dedication	3
Chapter 1	7
Chapter 2	10
Chapter 3	17
Chapter 4	26
Chapter 5	36
Chapter 6	56
Chapter 7	63
Chapter 8	74
Chapter 9	93
Chapter 10	102
Chapter 11	113
Chapter 12	116
Chapter 13	118
Chapter 14	122
Chapter 15	131
Chapter 16	136
Chapter 17	142
Chapter 18	146

Chapter 19	148
Author's Note	151

Chapter 1

My eyes blink open. Where am I? A haze blurs my vision. I rub my eyes to try and clear it. The sound of crackling and screaming in the distance. The smell of burning. I try to get up. I panic, trying to run. A face comes into focus.

"I need to get you out of here!" he shouts, grabbing my hand, his green eyes filled with fear, fear for me, his dark hair dishevelled. A loud crash rumbles the earth and throws us forward. Blood curdling screams everywhere.

I jump awake. Not again. This is the same nightmare I've had over the last two years. My body is tingling with goose bumps and a cold sweat is layering the top of my skin. I take a few deep breaths and swing my legs off the edge of the bed. I stand, stretching and rubbing my eyes. As I go to walk, I trip and fall with a thump.

"Toby! How many times have I told you not to sleep there!" I shout at the dog, rubbing my sore knee. He grumbles back in answer.

"Theadora? Are you awake? The movers will be here in an hour! I hope you've finished packing!" my mother shouts up the stairs.

Why does she always say my name like that? It's Thea. I look around my room. Boxes half packed, clothes all over the floor. Oops.
"Yeah mum! Almost done!" I start frantically throwing clothes into the suitcase. I lie on top of the suitcase, forcing it closed with all my might and stuffing any items back in as I zip it up. Once it's closed, I realise I've packed all my clothes and I'm still in my pyjamas. I quickly take out an outfit and stuff in my pjs. Thank god it's

my favourite hoodie. I pull it over my head and pull out my dark brunette hair. I look in the mirror. Freckles dotted over my nose and my eyes were dark blue today. I find they change shades a lot.

I pack up the rest of my room. The last things to be packed are my photos. I take them down off the wall, being careful not to drop the frames. I linger of over the image of my father. The picture was of a summer when I was eight. We were in the sea playing he was lifting me out of the surf. The memories flash through my mind like Polaroid snapshots. I smile and fight back the tears.

"You ready? Hey, I thought you said you were done?" my mum says walking into my room. She walks over and looks at the picture. "That was a good day." She says rubbing my shoulders affectionately. A tear escapes.

"Do you think he misses us?" I ask.

"I don't know Thea, I hope so. Wherever he may be," she says, disappointment slipping through her façade. "I'll help you finish. The van will be here soon."

I wrap the picture in tissue paper and place it delicately in the box. My father disappeared about two years ago. No calls, no messages, and hasn't accessed any money since. Police say they can't help us. My mother thinks he ran off with another woman. I heard her tell her friends one night. I can understand why. Before he disappeared, he was acting strangely, restless. I can't help but miss him though. I don't think he would do that to us. He wasn't like that. He loved us.

As we finish packing a horn blares outside.

"That'll be them," Mum says, and moves for the door. "I know you're not happy about this move, but your grandmother needs us. After her fall she needs a bit of help, and the job that I start there is better than the one here.'"

"I know, Mum. It's fine," I say, taping up a box.

We are moving from my childhood home in Cheshire to Pembrokeshire. My grandmother, my father's mother, has deteriorated since Dad disappeared. She thinks something bad happened to him. The doctors said that her mind has created a reality she believes to be real, to protect herself. She talks about Morgens, nymphs and witches, but the sentences don't make sense. She fell a couple of weeks ago and had been in hospital. The doctors said she will need help from now on.

We load the last of the boxes into the van. I step inside my home one last time. I take it in with a deep breath. The height chart on the doorframe. The love that once filled this house, the laughter, the warmth. Now a shell for the next family to fill.

"Come on, Thea. Time to go." She places her hand on my shoulder delicately. My mother is a beautiful woman, but the stress from my father disappearance had aged her. Her black hair dyed to hide the greys and her tired eyes always hidden behind her glasses.

We turned to the door and closed it behind us one last time.

Chapter 2

The drive was long. 4 hours. I stared out the window, stroking Toby's soft fur as we went. He was a Jack Russell with tan, white and black markings. He was scruffy most of the time, but after a trim it made him look mean. He lay down next to me, his paws on my lap, his tongue hanging out of his mouth. It *was* July. The temperature was warm, hotter in the car. I opened the water and poured a little in the bowl. He lapped it up happily.

"Are you excited for your new school tomorrow?" Mum shouts from the front of the car.

"Not really. There's only a week left. Not even a week, it's already Monday! I've done all my exams, so surely I can miss one week?" I plead again.

"The head teacher insisted. I'm sorry, honey. Just look at it this way, you may find some new friends for the summer! *And* you can invite them to your birthday party!" she says, doing a little excited dance.

"I'll be turning 18, no one will care to come to your annual party Mum. I don't even want to go to it this year!" I reply, annoyed. She always throws me the same party. I learned soon enough that the party wasn't for me. It was for her. To keep everything as normal as possible after Dad.

"Hey! What's wrong with my parties?" she says, offended with her hand on her chest.

"Just that they usually only consist of me, you and Toby since as my friends never wanted to go."

"Nick liked to come to the parties. He could come this year."

"Seeing as Nick is my ex-boyfriend; I have a feeling the answer is going to be a no." She always brought him up. She still can't believe I ended things after I found out we were moving a few months ago. It wasn't really a relationship anyway. We hardly saw each other, and this was my chance to give him his life back. Plus, I know he liked Rachel from Science anyway. They basically got together as soon as we broke up.

"You'll work things out I'm sure," she said, looking at me in the rear-view mirror.

"How about this year we just don't do anything? It won't be a bad thing. I just don't see the point in celebrating with a party."

"But it's you eighteenth!" she screeches.

"I know, but I just want to start this new chapter on a less embarrassing note than trying to get random strangers to come to a party."

She sat awkwardly. Pondering. I could see the shock on her face. She looked hurt but I couldn't keep having a party every year till I'm 50!

"Okay." She finally replies. "We will be there in about 20 minutes. Your Grandmother can't want to see you. She hasn't seen you in a few years... well in person." I FaceTime her sometimes even though she doesn't really get it. The amount of times I have been face to ear with her I can't even count.

We haven't been back in Pembrokeshire since the summer before a Dad disappeared. When the investigation was going on, she came to stay with us for a while but after a few months she had to go home and try to move on.

"Is she ever going to get better?" I ask.

"Her hip should be healed in a month or so, but she needs the support. She can't take care of herself like she used to. She needs us to be there for her in case anything happens again."

"That's not what I meant."

"The doctors said they are not sure. The mind is a marvellous thing. It can break just as easily as a bone though. They said some people sort themselves out, whilst others don't. So, we just need to hope."

I leaned against the door of the car, taking in the scenery. Beautiful rolling fields for miles, the sun casting its light through the clouds. Wildlife everywhere.

"Do you remember much of Stackpole? I know we used to come here every summer before Dad... but you lived here."
"Well, your father and I moved when we were 20, I found a job up in Chester and he came with me. He then found his job with the National Trust. It was a quiet village, not many people and beautiful beaches. My mother and father owned a farm not too far away. It kept us busy, before they passed. Your dad and I met at school, the one you will be going to. It's not as busy as the city but plenty of legends."

"I know fairies, sea monsters and witches. I remember the bedtime stories." I remember. I had always loved those. My dad would tell me of the three witches of the cliff, the mermaids and the fairies at Bosherston. He would tell it in so much detail it was like he truly believed. That's why it took me so long to get over the whole Santa Claus debacle. He was just so convincing!

"I know you do. There is a myth that King Arthur's castle is in Pembrokeshire." It feels like she is trying to sell me on the place.

"Cool." It was cool. I loved legends and myths. The fact that nobody knows what is true and what is not, it leaves a bit of mystery in world. My gaze drifts back to the window.

"We're here!" she shouts pulling up the handbrake on the car. I jump out and stretch my legs, raising my arms high in the air.

"Theodora, is that you?" a weary voice asks.

"It's me, Grandma." I say walking up to her to give her a hug. I do so gently, looking at the frail figure in front of me, one hand on a crutch.
"I'm so happy to see you. Len told me you were close."

"Len?" I ask, looking for a man in the house.

"Oh of course, this is Len," she says, pointing to the robin on the window ledge. Right, of course.

"Well, we are just going to unpack. Shouldn't you be sitting down?"

"I can't sit down all day! Your room is the attic room as you have the youngest legs!" she exclaims, pinching me on the bum as I turn.

Grandma's house was the same as I remembered it, just a little older. The white paint had started to chip off the walls and had green algae in some places. Inside was the same too. Oak floors, dressers, side tables with doilies draped over and vases with paper flowers inside. Old copper tea pot still placed on the top of the dresser with figurines on every surface. I looked down at the box in my hands. It was labelled kitchen. As I put the box down on the counter, I look at the shelves in front of me, top to bottom filled with spices and herbs, some I didn't even recognise. A pestle and mortar on the side of the granite worktop. Some vines had started to come through the kitchen window, and she had created a little area of an herb garden on the windowsill. Then I spotted it.

"Grandma, what is that?" I shout from the kitchen. She hobbles in after a few minutes.

"That's a protection charm for the house dear." She indicates to the mural she had painted on the back door, an intricate pattern of lines all joining together. This was getting a little creepy.

"To protect from what?" I ask hastily.

"Any being with evil intention. We don't want to end up like your father now do we?" she says matter of fact.

This was a trip. I took a long look at my grandmother. Her hair was crazy although weaved into a pretty bun while the rest of her long hair draped down. She wore her trusty medallion around her neck. She looked the same, I guess.

"Okay, well ill just get some more boxes. You sit down here and I'll make you a cup of tea." I fill the kettle and put it on the hob to boil.

I find one of my boxes and headed for the attic. I had never been in here before, and I can understand why. It's a little creepy. The stairs curl upwards surrounded by wooden walls on either side until I emerge in my new room. I try to switch the light on with no luck. I headed for the curtains and draw them open. It was bigger than I expected. The wooden floors creaked underfoot and a long built in wardrobe took up the far wall. The only other piece of furniture was an ornate, golden mirror decorated with vines and fruit. It was beautiful. As I looked at my reflection, I jumped slightly. It didn't look like me for a minute. Well, it did, but something was different… I'm starting to sound like Grandma.

Once all the boxes were in the correct rooms we sat down at the table for dinner. Mum had run out and got us a Chinese takeaway.

"It was thoughtful of you dear but there is plenty of food here," Grandma says.

"I know I just thought we would all be tired and it would save us cooking," my mother replied, dishing up the dinner onto the plates.

"I understand. Just make sure you check the food for curses. I'm not going through that again." She smiles, shaking her head with a chuckle.

As you can expect we ate in silence.

I headed upstairs after dinner and finished unpacking my clothes from the suitcase.

"Do you have your uniform for tomorrow?" my mum says poking her head up the stairs.

"Uh huh," I sounded, concentrating on folding my clothes.

"They did a great job putting your bed up," she says, pointing to the new bed in the middle of the room, "really goes with the place." It was a dark wood with spiral details on all four legs. Just what I had wanted. I'd dressed it with my favourite sheets. A garden design with greens, blues and golds covering it. Toby lay on top. Mum heads over to him, patting his head.
"I know you aren't thrilled about being here, but trust me, it's the best thing for your grandmother," she says apologetically. Again.

"I know, Mum. I just didn't realise how bad she had gotten. Did you see the back door?" Concern was lacing my voice.

"Really? That's what your worried about? That's normal for Gran! If anything, I feel like this is the best she has been in years," she replied laughing.

"That's normal?" I ask high pitched.

"Yup. She has always been a little witchy," she laughs, wiggling her eyebrows and her fingers.

"Like spells and curses?"

"More like nature and charms. You saw all the herbs? She used to make natural medicines and the odd potion. The animal chatter is new to me though."

"Oh, I feel like I barely know her."

"She did stop for a few years. She must have started back up I suppose. At least you can get to know her more now." She walks over to my uniform hanging over the mirror. "I'll iron these for you. You need to look your best," she says and heads back down the stairs.

Chapter 3

"You must be Theodora. I'm Mrs Scott, your Head Teacher." The lady in front of me threw out her hand for me to shake. She was a small woman, shorter than me, with her golden hair tied back into a neat bun. Her skirt suit neat as a button. I put my hand in hers. I could feel the stress in her hands, but her shake was firm.

"I'm Thea. Nice to meet you," I say.

"I'll escort you to your first class. As it is the final week of school, year 12 are working on projects as part of our extra curriculum. Your first lesson is History. They're working on a project based on Welsh Folklore."

We continued down the blue corridors, all covered with work done by pupils. No way was I going to navigate this place alone.

"Do you know any?" she asks.

"A little." I lied so I wouldn't have to talk to her. I needed to concentrate on where I was going. She opened the door. Everyone was already in their seats.

"This is Theodora Turner. She is a new student. Please make her feel welcome," the Head Teacher says, glaring at the entire class. I roll my eyes at the use of my full name.

"Hi Theodora. I'm Miss Russell. Would you like the to tell us a little bit about yourself?" she says. I was not ready for this part.
"Umm, hi, I'm Thea. I'm from Cheshire but my Gran lives in Stackpole. We moved here to take care of her, and I don't really know what else to say!" I look at the teacher awkwardly. She smiles. Her

glasses on top of her head.

"Okay Thea, why don't you take the empty seat next to Hali?" she says pointing to a smiling girl with long flowing blonde hair. She waved excitedly. Her eyes were bright blue. Something was strange though. I just couldn't figure it out.
I walked over and sat down.

"Hi, I'm Hali, like she said," she exclaims excitedly.

"I'm Thea, like she said." I reply, we both giggle a little awkwardly.

"What's your class schedule?" I take the folded piece of paper out of my backpack and hand it to her.

"We are in most of the same classes, except English Lit. You took that willingly?" she asks nose scrunched.

"I like it. What did you take?" I ask.

"Textiles," she says, pretending to whittle her pencil.

"Is there anything I need to know; you know like where not sit and all that?"

"Just stick with me, I got your back," she says with a wink.

I hung out with Hali all morning. She told me everything I needed to know. It was like we had known each other forever. I'm surprised we hadn't already made up code words for things. I'm joking. A little.

At lunch time we headed for the cafeteria.

"These are your new friends, Rose, Eva, Rowan and Finn," she says, pointing everyone at the table. My eyes moved over them, smiling at each but I couldn't help but stare at Finn. He stared right back.

"Do I know you?" he asks, standing with a hand outstretched to shake my own, smiling at me. He was almost exactly like my dream, down to the forest green eyes and ebony hair. Just something was different. Was I being crazy? How long had I been staring?

"Umm, hi. No I don't think so." I try to divert my gaze and look casual. "I'm Thea," I say, and put my hand in his. As our hands touched, images of my nightmare flooded my mind. I put a hand on my temple as if I was holding it in. His eyes lit up with recognition, but he diverted his gaze quickly, pulling his strong hand away from mine. Hali pulled me down to sit.

"So, Thea, tell us about yourself," he suggests, leaning over the table. His shoulders were muscular, his biceps even more so.

"She's not good at that." Hali stated, matter of fact.

"What do you want to know?" I ask.
"Why are you starting school now? It's a bit late in the year. I would have stayed a home," Eva says, smiling, clearly acting up for the group. She is a pretty girl. She has short dark hair and a fringe that just covers her left eyebrow.

"I was forced," I replied.

"Fair enough. Why Pembrokeshire?" Rose asks.

"My Grandma lives in Stackpole and needed help after a fall."

"What's her name?" Finn quizzed.

"Thea. Althea, I mean. A little bit eccentric, but it definitely suits her," I say with a giggle. They all look at each other. "Do you know her?" I ask puzzled.

"Yeah, she's my neighbour. I live a couple of streets over," Eva replies, looking weary.

"Cool. I guess."

Eva leans towards Rose and whispers maintaining eye contact with me. Oh god, they already think I'm weird. Thanks Gran.

"So, do you practice?" Rose asks, beraking away from the whispering. Her eyebrow raised, shooting me an *'I don't really care'* look. She was giving me the new girl treatment, her dark hair flowing down to her collar bone and dark eyes piercing me.

"Practice what?" I replied.

"See, I told you," Eva said under her breath, Hali elbowing her in the side. I play with my thumbs uncomfortably under the table.

"So where did you and your family live before?" Finn asks moving around the circular table towards me.

"Cheshire, and it's just me and my Mum. Where do you live?" I asked, trying to divert some of the attention off myself. I don't mind a little attention, but all eyes on me makes my face feel on fire.

"Close," he replie,s short and to the point. I shoot him a puzzled look; he sits in the empty seat next to me.

"I get it, just in case I'm crazy. I understand," I say jokingly.

"Ha-ha, you never know!" he says nervously. "Are you sure I don't know you?" he asks again, his ears twitching. That was weird. I could have sworn they were just pointed. He touched his ear nervously, his eyes still on mine. "How old are you?" he asks, when I haven't answered his first, or what feels like fifteenth question at this rate. It feels like I'm on an episode of who wants to be a millionaire. Topic: me.

"Seventeen. Eighteen in two weeks." He nodded in response.

"She smells like it though, right?" I overhear Eva whisper to Rose. She was definitely a bitchy person. Both of them, really. Finn drops his gaze from me to glare at Eva. She caught his glance and immediately shuts up and slouches in her chair defeated.

"Come with me." Hali demands standing. "Eva forgot to take her nice pills today." I fake a smile and follow suit. Eva went to argue, but Finn's gaze bore into her. She closed her mouth and continued to mope.

"I'm sorry about her, she doesn't mean to come across mean, she just doesn't have a filter sometimes," she apologises, as we walked into the bathrooms.

"Hali, do I smell?" I ask vulnerably.

"No, not like that," she laughs. Hard. "I can't really explain."

"Well I don't get it. I don't want to be the new, smelly, weirdo girl." I am trusting this stranger a little too much. I glance at my reflection in the mirror. This has been the strangest day. I look at Hali's reflection as she fixes her eye liner and it flickers slightly.

"Like I said not like that. Don't worry about it. Come on. Let's dash," she says, clearly finished with the conversation.

The rest of the school day I thought about Finn. How did he end up in my dream? Was it even him? How can I dream about someone I've never met? The questions swirling around my head while I sit in the classroom attempting to concentrate.

"You ready?" Hali asks at the end of school.

"For what?"

"To go home silly. I'll take you." She leads me to the back of school, Eva was waiting. "Hop in!" She had a bright turquoise blue Volkswagen Beetle. Definitely suited her personality.

"I'm sorry about earlier. I didn't mean any offence," Eva says apologetically. She held out her hand towards me. "Friends?"

"Friends." I replied taking her hand. I could feel her resistance, like she wasn't sure about me yet.

We hop in the car and Hali revs the engine like she's about to start a Formula One race. I resist gripping the arm rest, trying to not look like I am fearing for my life.

"So, do you have a boyfriend?" Eva asks, leaning between the seats from the back.

"No, you?" I reply, looking between them both.

They looked at each other, then, in unison, "No." Eva continues. "But there is this nym... nerd I had my eye on," she says as Hali shot her a look. Eva shrugs in response.

"What's his name?" I ask, confused by their silent conversation.

"Nathan," she smiles. "He's good with trees," she adds in a daze, clearly thinking about him. Trees though? That's a little weird. "Do you like anyone? I saw how you looked at Finn earlier. Shame he's already taken, " she remarks with a sharp tone that sliced through the air.
"Oh, no, I don't think so." I reply. I was a little pained to hear he had a girlfriend. He was literally the man of my dreams.

"What was that between you two? Do you know him?" she asked.

Well, I can't tell her about my nightmares, they'll think I'm crazy. "No just one of those faces I suppose."

"What devilishly handsome?" she replies, dreamily.

"Eva, don't be weird." Hali scolds.

"What? I can't lie," she admits, holding her hands in the air.
We pulled up outside my house. Thank god. That was the most awkward car journey of my life.

"See you tomorrow! Do you want a ride?" Hali shouts, leaning out of her window.

Well it does beat the bus. And I do want Hali to be my friend. "Sure. Thanks." I shout heading up the stone steps.
Grandmother was sat outside on the bench and waved as they drove away.

"You're friends with August's girl, Eva was it?" she asks.

"Sort of. She's a little bitchy," I reply honestly.

"She would be, she's the type," she giggles picking up her cup of herbal tea.

"Do I smell funny to you, Grandma?" I ask. It explodes from me. Like word vomit. It's been bugging me all day.

"Why would you ask that?" she asks turning towards me.

"Well, Eva said 'I smelled like one' to another girl and I just don't want to be that person, you know?" I state honestly.

"Well let's see." She breathes in deeply. "Earthy tones, fennel, lemon." She stopped abruptly. "Wait, let me put my tea down. That's all I can smell. Silly me." She turned to me again. Closing her eyes and breathing in deeply. She holds my hand. I feel slightly freaked out and want to pull away. "Lavender with hints of gladiolus, rue and…" she smacks her lips together. Her eyes shoot open. "Monkshood," she says, with a look of fear on her face.

"Does that smell bad?" I ask. What the hell is Monkshood? Sounds like a gross sort of mushroom.

"Come with me child, you need to see." I was getting more freaked out by the minute. She urges me on, shooing me into the house. We head towards the kitchen. "I promised I wouldn't say, but I never promised I wouldn't show. It's the monkshood I'm worried about." She lays her hand on my arm. "Sit there and wait."

"You're freaking me out. What even is monkshood?" I ask.

"It means a foe is near," she says as she hurries though her pots of herbs. I roll my eyes a little. "You've been having those nightmares haven't you." She looks at me over her shoulder. My eyes widened in disbelief. How did she know?
"Well, yes," I say, fear in my voice.

"What happens in them?" she asks hurriedly, constantly checking the door, putting all the herbs into the mortar.

"I'm not too sure, they are a bit blurry. They're just dreams. Fire and, well, Finn. From school," I say, wondering if I sounded crazy.

"You dreamt about him before you met him?" she asks.

"It's weird, I know," I replied. "I think I'm losing it," I add, rubbing my temples. She pours the kettle over the herbs and drains it into a teacup.

"This should help." She hands me the tea. It was teal in colour. I looked at it wearily. I sniffed. It smelt like a strong perfume. Florally.

"Is it safe?" I ask, wearily.

"Do you think I would try to kill you? It will help with the dreams and will help you see what is hidden." She leaned down to bring the cup to my lips. "Now drink up."

I drank as she requested. The tea was awful. It tasted of tree bark and it stung my lips. "Are there nettles in this?" I asked.
"Only a few. Trust me." I finished the cup. "Good. Now off to bed with you," she said abruptly waving her hands at me to hurry up the stairs.

"Bed? It's not even five o'clock yet? I'm eighteen for Christ's sake not eight!" I replied.
"Not for long. Just a quick nap. It will help the tonic," she insists, pushing me gently.

I did as I was told, my eyes starting to feel heavy as I ascend the squeaky stairs. As I get to my bed, my eyes start closing and fall backwards on to my soft mattress and everything turns black.

I fall hard with a thud on the floor. A blanket of heat comes over me. The grass underneath me cold and wet on my back. My ears ringing. I fight to open my eyes. Flashes of Violet across the sky.

A figure is coming. A desperate voice struggling to overpower the relentless ringing in my ears. "I need to get you out of here," Finn shouts, filled with worry. His fearful eyes staring into mine. He grabs my hand dragging me towards the tree line, the earth-shaking blast behind us and screams bellowing from the scene, blowing us to the ground.

"What was that?!" I shout over the ringing in my ears.

"The castle. They've taken the castle," he says, his eyes heavy with sadness, his face covered with soot, his hair dishevelled and his suit scorched. "Come on. We need to run." He pulls me to my feet. His hands are coarse against my skin. Pain shoots down my arm. Something flies towards me and then … darkness.

I wake in a sweat, gasping and scared. It took everything in me not to scream.

"It's alright dear." Gran said stroking my head. "What happened? What did you see?"

"Did you climb all those stairs? You're meant to be resting!" I shout, when I can finally breathe again.

"My hip feels as good as new, a few tonics did the trick. Now, what did you see?" she asks again.

"The fire, it was purple. Finn said something about them taking the castle, whatever that means. Why does it even matter? It is just a nightmare," I say puzzled.

"No dear, those are visions."

Chapter 4

"Visions. Okay Gran. You have had too many herbal teas today." She was getting worse.

"Okay then. Look at me. How do I look?" she asks, gesturing to her face. She looked the same. Her ears though. They were pointed and her hair more vibrant. A silver, rather than a grey. Her eyes gleamed blue. How hadn't I noticed this before?

"What did you give me?" I ask. I must be on a drug trip. She put cannabis in my tea or something. This must be how it feel to be high.

"A potion that lets you see what is being hidden. I hide this look to fit in. Your dreams … They started after your father… disappeared, correct?" she asks.

"Well yes, just grief I suppose." I rationalise.

"No. He was no longer around to give you the blocker," she says matter of fact.

"Blocker?"

"Your father. He was hiding your gifts from you. He didn't want you to know or anyone else to find out. You were too young," she says stroking my hair again, tucking the strays in neatly.

"This is too much Gran." I stand up to leave, she grabs my arm. "Don't your dreams feel real?" she asks.

"Well yes."

"Trust your instincts. It's what they're there for," she whispers.

I leave the house confused and head down road. I jump over the stile and head across a field, not really processing where I am walking, just concentration on the straight line. I keep going, my head pounding with questions. I end up with a pond in front of me. I kneel, dipping my fingers in the dark, murky waters, a run-down building on the other side. My face flushes as I struggle to keep my head from exploding. My eyes water with frustration. I lose track of time as I sit there gazing at the pond, scum masking what lies within the murky depths, processing the information. Was it true? Or was Grandma leading me down her loony road and I was just gullible.

"Can this be real?" I ask. As if understanding, a small frog jumps out depths and into the shallows in front of me. It sits there staring at me.

"Are you going to turn into a Prince if I kiss you?" I ask it, laughing at my stupidity.

"Maybe." The frog replied. I jump back in horror. My eyes bulging from my head. I turn running back across the field and towards my Gran's house. She was there, back on her bench, waiting for me to come home.
"How are you feeling dear?" she asks me, concern in her voice. She reaches a hand out for me to join her. Her appearance had not reverted back.

"Sceptical I suppose. Can I be honest with you?" I ask.

"I'd expect nothing less," she says, turning towards me on the bench.

"I don't know whether to believe you or not. The doctors said... If this was true, why didn't I know about it?" I ask.

"The doctors only know what they are told. I didn't want to go to those! Your Mother forced me, and I didn't want her to worry. My dear, this world is full of good. But it is also filled with evil. Bad people will do anything to get what they think they deserve. Our gifts are not of this world, but another that exists in harmony. Your dreams are just the beginning," she says, her eyes filled with compassion.

"But why don't I know about it then?" I ask, trying to push away the anger creeping into my voice.

"Your father's gift has been abused by others for many years, seeking things for people, memories, visions and objects that aren't supposed to be found. Word of his gifts spread and the bad came looking. I believe someone is keeping your father captive for them. He put a spell on you, a blocker, so no one would know of your gifts, not even yourself and when he disappeared, he was no longer able to renew the spell," she explains, looking towards the trees.

"What will happen to me?"

"Well, that depends on you. Your visions will be getting stronger now I have given you the tonic. Your dream is a warning of what is to pass. They may come true, they may not. You can work with me and I can teach you the ways of our ancestors, or you can have the spell renewed and ignore your fate," she states, making it obvious there was really only one choice.

"What will you teach me?" Her eyes light up.

"Well, I haven't had a student in a while, but first we would start with a bit of history, where you came from and about our kind. I will teach you potions and spells and then how to harness your gift so you can control it. You will be able to see what you want you and when you want to see it. Your gifts will grow from there. I don't know many half-bloods, but I would assume their powers would be different."

"Can we start now?" I ask. My mother's car comes into view and pulls up in front of the house.

"Tomorrow," she whispers just as my mother closes the car door.

∞∞∞

I headed for my room, trying to make sense of this revelation. It would be an explanation to what happened to my father. But the dream? Why was Finn in it? As I get to the top of my stairs, I hear Toby growling. He is sat in front of the mirror staring. I grab a sheet to cover it, but my face, it looks different. My ears were slightly pointed! Not as much as Grans, but still! My hair looked darker than before, full of life. I touched my face and then the mirror. It rippled like water on a pond. I pull my hand back with a flash. What the hell was that? The reflection changed to the image of a room. The image rippling like a flag in the wind. The large room was quite bare but full of shadowy corners. A table sat in the centre of the room with items scattered across. Open books, bottles, a candle. I slowly move my hand toward the mirror and touch it once more. It was going through. I push a little further following my hand through. I close my eyes as my head goes through. The feeling of submerging my face in jelly before I emerge through to the other side.

I turned to see if the mirror was still there. An identical one hung on the wall, showing Toby leaning against the mirror looking for me. The room was different to how it looked in the mirror. It was round for starters and the light beamed in from a window, leaving shadowy corners dark and creepy. The walls were covered in marble and the floor made of a beautiful gold mosaic tile. Where the hell am I? As I head for the window, the immense landscape unfolds in front of me. I am really high up. A door behind me creeks open.

"What are you doing here?" I turn towards the shocked voice.

"Finn? What are you doing here?" I ask, clearly confused.

"This is my home. How did you get here?" I glance at the mirror, feeling too crazy to say it out loud, and he nods in recognition.

"Thinking about me, were you?" he asks, smiling.

"Excuse me?"

"Well, that mirror, it takes you were you want to go. Where there is a mirror, that is. Not many of its kind anymore. I take it your Grandma has one," he says, walking towards me. I nod in response. "You look different." He walks around me slowly. "I see the spell is broken." He was different too. His eyes were a more vibrant emerald his ears pointed too. I never realised how tall he was. His broad, muscular shoulders towering me. His chiselled jaw, shaping his handsome face. I let out a little gasp. He was beautiful.

"I'm sorry. I shouldn't be here. I just sort of fell through," I lied trying to make a good excuse.

"It's fine. You know who you are then?" I nod once more.

"Not that I fully believe it yet." I shrug glancing back out the window. "Where am I exactly? This doesn't look like Stackpole." He laughs, wholeheartedly.

"We are in the Seelie Court. Come with me. I have something to show you." He opens the door. I hesitate and then follow him anyway.

The corridor led to a set of winding stairs. At the bottom was a brightly lit corridor. The setting sun was shining over the balcony. Vines were clinging to the beams and bright colourful flowers draped over the side. The smell of the place hits me like a wave. A smell I have never smelt before.
"What is that?" I said pointing to my nose. "That smell?"
"Magic." He raises a hand and a vine comes to meet it. A flower blooming in his hand. "Light magic, to be precise. Here," he says handing me the flower. I take it, trying to hide my cheeks. He continues into the next building, and into a small room to the side.

Rowan, Eva, Rose and Hali are all sat their waiting. A small sitting room with a gold ornate sofa, facing a large decorative fireplace, made from slate, I think. Symbols carved into it.

"I knew I could smell it on you," Eva said with the cocky smile of confidence.

"Yeah, yeah we know. But it wasn't your place to spill the beans," Hali said pointing at her. Eva sticks out her tongue in response.

"How can you smell it?" I ask.

"It's unique to all Fae. Put it this way, you didn't smell human. They smell like sweat and sugar. You'll learn the difference," Eva said pulling a face like she was going to vomit. They all roll their eyes at her.

'So, what are you?' I ask trying not to sound offensive.

"I'm a Morgen, or a sea nymph," Hali replied. "Little Miss 'I Know everything' over there is a pixie. Meaning she likes to be a dick," she laughed.

"Hey!" Eva shouted, hitting Hali in the arm. "Rose is a wood nymph and so is Rowan. Collectively, we are Seelie." I look at them all in turn. Rose staring at me, not saying a word.

"So, what are you?" I ask turning to Finn.
"Royal." Eva smiles throwing the word at me. "Finn is a Prince, if you hadn't guessed already." I looked at them shocked. Finn throws a glare at her, but she ignores it.

My eyes pop from my head. "Wait, this is your castle?" he nods. Why didn't I realise this before?

"Don't get ahead of yourself, sugar, he's betrothed."

"Eva, shut up!" he shouts, his glare burrowing into her.

"Better she knows now, save her the hassle of getting her heart broken," she shrugged.

31

"You seriously need to work on your people skills," Rowan says, throwing one of the plush cushions at her.

"Don't hate on the truth." She waves her hand in the air and creating a halo over her head.

"So, who are you engaged to? Aren't you too young?" I ask, hoping I didn't overstep.

"Brighid, the Princess of the Unseelie. They are trying to join the two realms through marriage. It is my duty to the kingdom to end the war," he replies, not making eye contact with any of us.

"Anyway, we had better be going." Hali hurries Rowan, Rose and Eva out the room. "Plenty of homework." Eva goes to argue, and Hali clicks her fingers and she is only able to croak, as she shoves her out the door.
"I should be going too," I say, half curtsying as I leave. He chuckles. I look around. "How do I get back?" I ask.

"First, come with me." He directs me to the door in the corner of the room, opening the beautifully carved door with a huge tree carved into it, painted with gold. "Is this you?" he questions, pointing to the drawing on the desk. I glance over and sit down at the large solid dresser. It was me. Outside my old house.

"How do you have this?" I ask a little freaked out.

"I saw you in a dream. I keep seeing you and I don't know what it means. I know where you are. I could feel you here when you arrived." He runs his hands through his hair.

"It feels a bit like an invasion of privacy," I said under my breath.

"I'm sorry I didn't mean to freak you out, it's not exactly voluntary, but I have a feeling you know me too." He moves to sit on the edge of his grand bed. I turn in the chair to face him.

"I see your face in the same dream. Never in others. There's a fire, and we are running from something. It's not really clear."

"You have visions?" he asked. "Can I see?" He holds out his hand to me and I take it. "Think about the dream," he says and closes his eyes. I can't help but look at him. His nose wrinkles and his brow furrows as he tries to concentrate. I close my eyes too so I can see the dream. After a minute or so he opens his eyes. "That's some nightmare. Do you see anything else?" he asks desperately.

"No that's it. I only saw it clearly for the first time today. How can you see my dream?" I reply, feeling bad that I can't help more.

"Because you let me," he smiles, showing my hand in his. He lets go of my hand, realising he is still holding it. He looks at me and smiles. "You're different to how you are in my dreams."

"How so?" I ask.

"Well, I can't really explain it," he says smiling.

"I suppose you're different too. Less life and death." He let out a small smile. Shit, maybe I shouldn't have said that. I've made it a little awkward. "I think I should go now." I head towards the door. "Can you take me back to the mirror?"

"Sure." He gets up and leads the way.

"Do you want to get married?" I ask, trying to make conversation. "To the Princess, I mean." Really Thea duh?

"Does anyone want to marry someone they haven't met?" he shrugged.

"I suppose not." I sigh. "Can't you say no?"

"Duty over Love. That's what my father tells me anyway. My mother has been planning it for over a year." He walks beside me, our shoulders brushing together.

"Well, she will be lucky to have you," I smile, nudging him with my shoulder. Was that too much?

"Thanks. She would be luckier to have someone who loved her." I can't argue with that.

"Phineas!" A voice shouts from behind. "You are meant to be in a suit fitting. Who are you?"

"Mother, this is Thea. From school," he says awkwardly.

"Your other friends left earlier, why is she still here?" the stern woman glowered down at me, a golden woven circle sitting perfecting on her head. The Queen. Her hair was golden and flowing down towards her green dress.

"I was just leaving. I'm sorry, your highness," I say, trying to do a small curtsy, but Finn holds me up.

"Why are you heading to the Seer tower?"

"That's the way she came in," Finn replies. "She is Althea's Granddaughter."

"Oh." Her demeanour changes instantly. Softer, her brow unfurls, and she takes a step back. "I'm sorry, I didn't realise she had a Granddaughter."

"My father was Rhys," I replied. Her eyebrows raise in shock.
"I'm sorry about your father, dear."

"How did you know him?"

"He worked for us. He was the Seer to the Kingdom. He never mentioned he had a daughter though. When he disappeared, we looked everywhere but there was no trace to follow." She looked at me apologetically. "Anyway, it was nice to meet you, but you must be headed off. Finn is getting married in two weeks," she says with a false smile, pinching his cheeks a little. She turns and leaves.

"Why didn't you tell me?" I ask turning to Finn.

"I didn't realise he was your father. Now quick, before she comes back. She will have me married tomorrow if I disobey her!" he mocks with an awkward laugh. He hurries me up the stairs and back into the tower room. Falling on the last step, he grabs my hand and pulls me towards him. I feel a buzz on my skin where I touch him.

"You look better this way," he says looking at my ears. "It suits you." He pushes a strand of hair out of my face. My stomach fills with butterflies and I make a gulping noise. Does he feel this too? Realisation sets in his eyes and he pulls his hand away, but he doesn't let me go. "Thank you for coming," he smiles.

"You're welcome. Even though I didn't actually mean to come." I glance up at his eyes and down to his lips. They were full and kissable. I shook my head and focused. He was a little to close but I liked it. His warmth seeping into me, hesitantly, I pull away, his eyes following me as I go. He's getting married in two weeks.

"So, do I just think of my room?" I ask. He fumbles and takes a step back against the wall.

"Uh, yeah," he says, making sure there is plenty of space between us.

"Thank you. I'll see you tomorrow?" I ask placing my hand on the mirror.

"Definitely." As the mirror starts to pulls me through, a thought strikes me. "What date is your wedding?"

"The 24th, why?" he said, his jaw clenched.

"Oh no, reason." I lied and stepped through the mirror. I shake my head as I get to my bedroom. Of course, he would be getting married on my birthday.

Chapter 5

I had to slip into my grandma's room after my mother went to bed. She was waiting for me in her chair by the window.

"Are you ready to listen?" she asked, placing a book down on her oak side table.

"Definitely," I reply, sitting on the edge of her bed.

"Let me start by saying, your father didn't keep this from you to be mean. He was trying to protect you. And your mother has a spell on her to forget. It was the only way for you to be safe after your father disappeared." She leans towards me. "I hear you went through your mirror?"

"How did you know?"

"I heard the buzz of the magic when you slipped through. We used to live in the fae realm. Your grandfather, father and I, but after your grandfather died, I couldn't stay. We needed a fresh start, with less magic."

"Less magic?" my brow furrowed in confusion.

"There is less magic in this realm, meaning in my grief I had more control. We always planned on returning, until your father met your mother. Humans cannot cross into the Fae realm. Your father chose to stay with your mother. Without him, there was no reason for me to return. Where did you go? When you went through the mirror, I mean."

"Finn's castle," I reply, awkwardly.

"Interesting. So, you saw the other realm for yourself?" she asked moving to sit next to me on the bed.

"Just the Castle. Eva, Rose, Hali and Rowan were there. I wasn't there long. Why do you have the mirror?"

"I used to work for the palace as a healer, so when I moved to this realm, I took it with me and used it to collect herbs and ingredients I wouldn't find here. Your father used it then when he became the Seer. He was a powerful man. The same gift you have, but I'm sensing not the only gift," she says, placing her hand on mine. "Funny how you ended up friends with a group of Fae. Though I have never heard of Rose before. I wonder who her parents are?" she ponders to herself. "The ties of fate are pulling you hard' I see."

"Do you know what other magic I have?" I ask. She grips my hand.

"No, but that will all come with time. Tomorrow I will teach you about the potions. But for now, you need your rest." She places her hand on my forehead. "There, hopefully you won't have any visions tonight." I head for the door and turn to look at Gran, who had just started to get into bed.
"Gran, I feel terrible that I never believed you. You let everyone think you were crazy."

"All the best of us are dear," she says, paraphrasing Alice in Wonderland, a book she used to read to me before bed. "Now, goodnight." Gran smiles at me as I leave.

She was right. I slept like a log. As I opened my eyes, I saw Toby is stood, staring at me.
"Really? You're freaking me out." I state and as if understanding, he got up and walked downstairs. My ears twitched when I caught a faint humming sound. I slide off the bed searching for the sound, swaying around looking for the hum to get louder. I end up facing the mirror once more. It has never hummed before. I touched the mirror and a flash moved across, as if someone was running out of view. Freaked out, I covered it over with my blanket and rush

downstairs.

Gran was already in the kitchen, clipping rosemary from her small herb garden on the windowsill.

"Sleep well dear?" she asked, without turning.

"Can people look through the mirror into my room?" I question, in panic.

"Only if they have the same one," she says with a shrug. "Why?"

"Well I woke up to it humming and when I looked, something moved," I stressed.

"Right. I will put a ward on it. That's the last thing we want is people watching or wandering in here! Here let me show you how to make it." She grabbed the mortar from the side. "This can be your first lesson. Potions can be powerful things and dangerous in the wrong hands. Like magic. There is light magic and dark magic."

"How do you know the difference?" I watched as she grabbed a few jars of herbs of the shelf.
"The smell mainly. Good magic smells good, like nature, grass, herbs, flowers, honey, the sea, the wind, the rain etc. Dark magic smell rotten. People who use dark magic are usually identifiable by their looks. There are a lot of spells and potions to hide these though. You," she points at me, "will be able to feel it. Your instincts protect you. The gift of sight protects you." She covered my eyes with her hands.
"What does your instincts tell you about me?" she asks. "Not how you think of me but the feeling I give you when you think about me." I think for a moment.

"You're my Gran," I say not really knowing what she means. She uncovers my eyes.

"Okay, okay. Close your eyes. Try... Hali."

"I feel I can trust her. She makes me feel like she's got my back."

"Good. I'm glad. Now Eva."

"She's brutally honest. I can't trust her with secrets I know that, but she feels like a good person overall."

"Last one. Finn?" my eyes fly open in a panic. "Go on." She waves her hands for me to proceed.

'Well, I feel drawn to him. I don't know if it's the dreams but there is something there. I can trust him. I can count on him. I feel safe when I'm with him." I open my eyes and she's grinning at me with one of those 'how cute' grins. I hit her playfully in the arm. "Stop it!"

"The heart wants what the heart wants," she sings rhythmically.

"He's getting married."

"I don't change my argument," she giggles. "Right Thea. Head in the game. These are the herbs you will use in most spells. Like a building bricks of all potions…" lifting each one in turn telling me why she adds each herb to the potion. She adds the ingredients to the mortar and hands it to me.

"Now grind. But while you do. You need to think what you want this potion to do," she says, picking up the used jars and placing them back in their original place.

"Why?"

"The magic of the potion comes from you. The intentions will flow through you and into the potion." I nod with understanding. "How do I know if it works?" and as if to answer my question a small plume of pink glittery smoke spouts from the bowl. "Oh, never mind. I must admit, that felt good!"

"It's ready." Follow me.

We headed up to my room. "Why doesn't Mum ask about your hip? Surely she thinks it's weird that its already better?"

"I use the crutch when she's around," she says raising a finger to her lips.
As we take the winding stairs to my attic room, we hear a rustle then the hum of the mirror. I run up the stairs to catch someone. But the room is empty.

"Someone was in here," I say when my Gran emerges from the staircase.

"Does anything look out of place?" she asks, scanning the room. It was a mess. Half empty boxes, clothes still half put into the drawers.

"I don't think so." A little embarrassed, it's not like I would be able to tell anyway.

"Seems whoever was watching, did fancy a visit. Not a moment too soon for this potion." She dips a paintbrush in and sweeps it over the mirror. It glows for a minute then returns to normal. "There," she says, leaning back to look at her handy work. "Now only you will be able to leave and return as the potion contains your magic. No one will be able to look through either, which is definitely a good thing." She steps away and glances around the room. "You could do with a brownie to clean up after you. The small creature that cleans not the sweet, chocolatey snack," she laughs, reading my confusion. "Now get ready for school. You only have a little while until Hali gets here," she says, nodding to the Robin outside the window.

The horn honks outside and I run down to the car.

"Before you go dear, drink this. It hides the ears." She thrusts a glass into my hands. It surprisingly tastes nice, citrussy.
"Come on!" Hali shouts from the car.

I run and hop in the front. "No Eva?"

"I think we could both do with the morning off from her." I nod in agreement. "She doesn't mean to come off so hostile. It's just her way. How are you dealing with it all?"

"A bit of an information overload. My head was killing last night. I feel better about it all today."

"That's good. I can't imagine what it feels like to only just find out who you are. Do you have any questions I can help with? I'm somewhat of an expert on all things fae." Hali says, placing her hand to her chest, pretending to be modest.

"What magic do you have?" I ask.

"Good question. I have power over the water. I grow gills when I'm in there. But, there are good and bad of us though. Me, I just worship the water. There are others such as sea hags, mermaids and sirens. They use their power to lure people to their deaths. I would only do that if someone really pushed me to it," she says with a shrug. "Speaking of mermaids- fancy going to the beach tonight? We're all going. Should be fun."

"But it's a Wednesday?" She looks at me over her sunglasses.

"And your point is?" Damn, I sound like a child worrying about school nights.

"Sounds good!" I reply trying to sound a little cooler.

"That's the spirit! I'll take you back to yours after school and you can pick up your stuff for swimming."

As we pull into the carpark at school Eva and Rose walk towards the car.

"Nice of you to join us," Eva remarks.

"Bite me." Hali replies.

"So, Thea. How are you finding school so far?" Rose asks a fake smile spreads across her face.

"Great thanks. Nice to have some friends already I guess." She smiled again but her eyes said otherwise.

"I invited her to our beach trip later." Hali says, gathering her bag from the trunk.

"Oh, I didn't realise everyone was coming." Rose grimaced.
"If everyone is us five then yes, we are all coming," Hali replies. The bell sounds and we head towards our classrooms. Eva and Rose head off in the opposite direction towards theirs.

"You seem to get under her skin," Hali said, hiking her thumb over her shoulder, I presume to Rose.

"Did I do something to piss her off?"

"I don't know. She's a little strange, to be fair. She started school about a year ago and has been stuck to Eva ever since. Plus, she does have a thing for Finn, but he ignores it trying to be nice." She takes a piece of gum from her bag and offers me the packet. I take a piece and smile. "Actually, that's probably why she doesn't like you." She nods with understanding.

"What? Why?" I ask surprised.

"Do you think I'm an idiot? I saw how you two acted yesterday. He clearly likes you," she chewed.

"He's engaged," I said, holding up my right hand as if to show off a ring.

"The heart wants what the heart wants," she shrugged.

"You sound like my grandma." She laughed at that.

"I can see the sparks. You would have to be blind not to." She closed her eyes feeling the air in front of her. "Oh, my mistake. I can still feel them anyway." She laughed. I hit her with my bag.

"You are seriously not funny."

"It's okay, your secrets are safe with me," she laughs, putting pinched fingers to her lips and zipping them closed.

"All of them?" I ask, even though I can already feel I can, I like to make sure.

"I guess, why do you have more?" she asks as we enter the classroom, tapping her fingers together like a movie villain.

"Maybe some other time." I gesture to the full classroom.

Lunch comes around quickly as we head to the cafeteria. "So, dish me those secrets," Hali says urgently, leaning towards me as we walk.

"Well—" I trip, falling face first to the cold linoleum floor. Just before my nose makes contact with the hard ground, somebody grabs my flailing arms and yanks me back up. The electricity that spas through my skin lets me know who it is before I look up and meet those brilliant emerald eyes.

"We seriously have to stop meeting like this." Finn jokes. My gaze moves from the floor to his face and his eyes are smiling.

"I'm sorry, I'm such a klutz," I say, shaking my head.

"It's okay, I think I like catching you." I lean back and step away from him.

"Thanks, I guess." I turn around to see what I tripped on. Eva and Rose were sat at the next table, laughing. I try to hide the embarrassment on my face.

"Come on let's get something to eat," Hali suggests, holding my arms and moving me towards the queue. "We will be over in a minute guys," she shouts over her shoulder.

"Okay, that was like fireworks," she said, placing a finger to my arm and shaking it like I burned her.

"She tripped me up," I said angrily.

"Who did?" she said looking around. She catches sight of Rose and Eva sniggering at me.

"Oh fates no," she said waving her hand. "I'll fix this." She points a finger towards the girls and as they go take a drink of their water, she flicks her wrist. The water cup overturns on their faces, soaking them.

Hali quickly turns to me. "Don't look. They'll think it was you," she said, giggling under her breath.

"I think you just started Girl War 3 I'd say. They are going to hate me." I said, trying not to look at them, but couldn't help smiling.

"Totally worth it." She erupts in laughter, quickly covering her mouth with her hand. As I finally take a look at the table, Rowan is laughing hysterically. I turn to Finn who is staring at me smiling.

"I think he knows it was us," I whispered to Hali.

"No, I think he just likes you."

"You think?" I asked not dropping my gaze from his.

"Well, now I know you like him," she says, laughing. She waves her hand at me. "Come on love bird," She giggles as we head down the queue.

After school we headed to my house. "What do I need?"
"Bikini, a drink, some sun cream ... have you not been to the beach before?" she asks with sarcasm in her tone.

"I like to be prepared," I reply putting the stuff into a bag.

Hali looks around my room. Grandma must have come up and finished emptying the boxes. My room was spotless and looked so much bigger.

"Is this the mirror you came through yesterday?" she pointed at it, still stood in the corner.

"Uh huh," I mumble, throwing the bag over my shoulder.

"You ready?" she asks turning to look at me.

I had put on my red bikini, with a white kaftan covering it, but still see through.

"Is that for Finn?" she asks with a smile and wiggle of her brows. It was my best bikini. It showed off my breasts and small waist.

"No." I replied, my cheeks pinking a little. She shook her head as if she didn't believe me. "So, what beach are we going to?" I ask, trying to change the subject.
"Freshwater West. Best beach around. I hope you've packed some warmer clothes for later," Hali laughs as we head down the stairs and to her car. I nod and we wave goodbye to Gran.

A small car park is situated by the colossal sand dunes, the sand dusting itself across the road. Long reed-like grass covers the dunes. Eva and Rose were already there. We pull the deck chairs from the boot and toss the bags over our shoulders.

"Nice outfit," Eva says. Her fringe is blowing in the wind. She is wearing a purple t-shirt and denim shorts. Eva has a black bikini top with a black jacket half zipped up.

"Thanks," I reply, feeling her words are sincere. Out of nowhere Finn and Rowan come up behind Hali and I and take the stuff out of our hands.

"Can't have you pretty ladies carrying anything to strenuous, now can we?" Rowan remarks, his blonde hair a little longer than it should be, blowing almost perfectly in the breeze, and looking intently at Hali, her blonde hair flowing just over her blue bathing suit.

"Thanks!" I shout. Finn turns and winking in reply. I turn to Hali. "So, Rowan, huh?" I say, nudging her with my elbow as we head through the dunes towards the beach. The sand seeps into my flip flops, and I shake it out quickly as the sun-drenched grains burn my heels.

"Only forever," she sighs, "but don't tell the other girls. They would only use it against me."
"Your secrets are safe with me," I laugh, mimicking her lip zipping.

"Thanks, it's nice to feel I have true friend around." She smiles and links my arm.

"Me too." We smile at each other and head for the shore.

The beach stretched for miles, a pebble bank near the base of the dunes, the rest of the beach, pure gold. The tide was going out as the water drenched grains sparkles in the afternoon sun. The mirrors of water reflecting the brilliant blue sky.

The boys had already started for the rockier side of the beach. "Shouldn't we stay on the sand? It will be much nicer," I ask Hali.

"Just you wait," she says, pointing to them. With a flash, they disappear.

"Where did they go?" I ask, looking around. She laughs and breaks into a run.

"Come on!" she shouts. As we near the jagged rocks there is still no sign of the boys. "Come here and hold my hand." I take it and she leans down to the rock in front of her. It did look oddly out of place on the beach. Minimal signs of erosion from the harsh sea and a small intricate carving on the front. As she touched it and a force sucked us through the stone.

I tried to stay standing but felt a bit dizzy.
"Sorry, I forgot to tell you about that. The first time always sucks." She griped my arms to steady me.

"What was that?" I asked placing a hand on her shoulder for support.

"A portal to the Seelie Realm. As I said, Best Beach." She points out to the view. The sea looked brighter, deep turquoise and clear; the sand softer under my feet, cool even. The waves crashed against the rocks near the cliff face, creating our own miniature rainbows. The best part of all? No one else around. "Our secret spot," she beamed, running straight for the ocean diving into the waves.

"Like a moth to a flame, that one." Rowan gestured, laughing. A second later, Rose and Eva appear.

"More like a fish out of water!" We all laugh. "She looks lonely out there. Maybe we should join her?" I suggest.

"Don't have to tell me twice," he says taking off his t-shirt and running to the sea.

"Come on," I call to Finn and the girls. Finn took off his shirt in answer. A little squeak escapes my throat at the sight of his muscles. I turn feeling a little embarrassed and start to take off my Kaftan. The girls did the same all of us running for the great wide sea. As I jump into my first wave the cold hits me in the chest and I let out a little gasp.

"Come on Thea. It's not that cold!" Hali jokes. Since entering the water her hands had developed some webbing and small gills on her chest. Her skin was almost iridescent and slightly blue.

"I'm sorry I don't have witchy water magic!" I shouted back, splashing her.

"Wrong game to play," she says, and sends a wave towards me. I submerge myself to prevent being thrown down the beach.

I swim out to the group, getting used to the chill against my skin. More refreshing than freezing now.

"Nice dodge," Hali winked. We were just out of our depth. Rose and Eva were staying close to Finn and Rowan.

"Any cool things you can do?" I ask pointing, to her newly grown flippers.

"I can breathe under water, hence the gills. I can swim fast. Oh! And this." She dives under the water and about 300 yards away soars out of the water and flips, spinning the water in the air like a Catherine wheel.

"Wow!" Rowan gasps, high fiving Finn.

I rise my legs up in the water to float. Staring into the sky, breathing in the salty sea air. Drifting in the waves. I get lost in the relaxing feeling of weightlessness. No thoughts of worries of annoyances.
"Thea!" A faint voice beckons to me. I turn to look and realise I have drifted too far, headed towards the cliff. I start to swim back to them, but I feel something slowly wrap around my ankle, one tendril at a time. I struggle to break free, the grip getting tighter.

"Hel-!" I scream just before it drags me under. I open my eyes to see what has got me. A green slimy hand around my ankle, dragging me into the abyss. The hair like seaweed drifting in the ocean. The head turns to me.

"Princess will be most pleased," the monster screeches, black eyes like the deep pits of hell. I don't know if the fact I could hear her underwater, or the fact she was trying to drown me, freaked me out more. I can feel the evil within her seeping into my ankle like the cold chill of winter, where she holds it. My lungs burn as I struggle to hold my breath. My eyes feel heavy. Deeper and deeper into the sea. Weakness taking over my limbs to the point where I can no longer fight.

I feel a hand grip my arm trying to pull me away. I blink to see another hand grabbing the other arm. A blast of water hits the Sea Witch with unrelenting force. She loosens her grip enough for the strong arms to pull me to the surface. As the surface breaks around my head I gasp in the sweet, crisp air above, coughing and spluttering like an old petrol lawnmower.

"Are you okay?" Finn grips me in his arms wiping the hair out of my face. I must look so attractive right now.

"What the hell was that?" I say, gasping in the air my lungs craved.

"A Sea Hag. They shouldn't be in this realm," he replies. "Can you track her Hali? I'm going to transport to the castle and get the Sea Guard."

"On it," she shouts, flipping her tail in the air as she goes.

"Rowan, take the girls back.'" He points at Rose and Eva. "Hold on okay?" Finn wraps my arms around his neck. He closes his eyes and the air buzzes around us, and in a flash, we were at the castle, a gush of water dispersing over the stone floor. My head felt woozier with the travel. Finn placed me down gently on a nearby bench. "Stay here."
He walked over to the shocked guard paddling in our sea water. Immediately the guard nods and walks away.

"How did you do get us here?" I ask, my head spinning.

"Transportation magic. Comes in handy if you need to get out of somewhere quick. Can you walk?" he asks, not waiting for an answer and swooping me up anyway, his warmth radiating into me, making me melt inside. "Never mind. This will be quicker."

"Thanks again." I say embarrassed.

"The third time now is it? I'll have to start charging," he laughs. We head down a golden corridor and up the stairs curling towards the sky.

"I have feeling the bill will be a long one the way I'm going," I chuckle nervously. "Do the sea hags have royalty?" I ask.

He looked puzzled by the question. "Why would you ask that?"

"Well when she was dragging me down, she said 'The princess will be pleased'. I assumed she was taking me to her sea hag Princess."

"The only Princess she would obey is one who was paying her. The

Unseelie Princess." Anger flashes across his face.

"Your fiancée ? Why would she want me dead? How would she even know me?" I shook slightly with panic. His grip tightened.

"Don't worry. I got you," he said looking at me with eyes so dreamy. We entered the sitting room next to his bedroom. Finn sat down on the sofa placing me next to him. "First we need to get you warm," he said rubbing my arms. He holds out his hands to the golden fireplace igniting the fire with a blast. "How are you feeling?" he asks.

"Honestly? A little naked." He leans away to look at me, like he couldn't remember what I was wearing, his gaze lingering a little too long. He blinks himself out of his daze.

"Right, one second." He went into his bedroom and returned with one of his shirts. He sat back down, wrapped it around me doing the buttons up slowly. I know I could do them up myself, but I enjoyed him doing it so much more. "How about now?"
"Like Pretty Woman." I giggle, the reference going completely over his head, his eyes confused. "You have never seen the film Pretty Woman?" I ask shocked.

"I haven't seen many films," he shrugged.

"Well that is a must see, a classic!" my hands emphasising the word.

"Maybe you could show it to me sometime?" he says, leering down at me. I gulped.

"Definitely. When you... have some free time." I struggle to get out the words. My eyes switching between his eyes and his lips. Suddenly, he leans down and presses his lips to mine. Heat erupting between us. My heart thundering in my chest, like it was ready to take flight. My skin heating at his touch. When reality hit me like a ton of bricks, I slowly pushed him away.

"You're getting married in less than two weeks," I almost whisper.

He looks away, cheeks flushed with the heat. "I don't want to marry her," he says.

"What do you want?" I ask, biting down hard on my lip.

"You," he whispers, turning to look at me, his green eyes burning into my soul. My heart thumps against my rib cage, like it's just learning what it's beating for. "I can't get you out of my head. Before we met you were just a dream. A perfect girl that I wanted," he says, sweeping a strand of hair behind my pointed ears, his hand lingering on my cheek. "Now you're here and I can't stop thinking about you."

"Finn, what about everything you said yesterday? The duty to your kingdom?" Why was I fighting this? I want him; I just didn't want to stand in his way. His jaw tightens. A guard enters, faltering at the door from interrupting.

"Your Highness, there is no sign of the sea hag." He said. Finn's fist clench and he hits the ornate table. The guard still lingers at the door.

"What?!" Finn shouts, the guard taking a step back.

"Your friends are here, your highness. Shall I send them in?" the guards eyes flicking from me to Finn. He waited a minute, looking back at me. Before he could say a word, Hali erupts into the room.

"Thea!" she said jumping onto the sofa between us and hugging me. Finn stands, moving to the back of the sofa, leaning against it. Eyes still on me. I send him a sorry look. "I tried to follow her, but she disappeared just beyond the portal. Those sea hags are always making us morgens look bad." Finn nods a thanks.

Rose, Eva and Rowan sweep into the room.
"Are you okay?" Rowan asks, sitting next to Hali.

"Yeah thanks to you lot. That was a pretty awesome blast Hali." I pushed her softly in thanks.

"I can't believe she thought she could enter our realm. What did she want with you?" she asks.

"Apparently the Princess sent her."

"That Unseelie bitch. I told you she was bad news Finn! When I see her, I'm going to show her how we Seelie say an Unseelie hello. A kick in the teeth!" she fumes.

A tension fills the room, a dark cloud. I look for where it is emanating. Eva and Rose. Something was definitely up. Hali follows my gaze.

"And where the hell were you two?" she shouts, standing, pointing at them aggressively. "She could have been sea bait and you two were gone!" Rowan stands up and puts his hands on her shoulder.

"Come on, Hali, it wasn't their fault. Let's go for a walk." He leads her out of the room, well, pulls her.

"I think I should go home now." I say, looking back up at Finn.

"I'll take you to the mirror." He slides around the edge of the sofa and offers me his arm. Eva and Rose glare at me as he does so, the cloud of tension filling all spaces. He helps me up and I offer him a thankful smile.

As we entered the hallway the calm air soothed me. "Did you feel that?" I asked.

"No, what?" he asked. I felt silly, like perhaps I was reading too much into things.
"Never mind." I replied. Luckily, he never questioned any further. As we reach end of the corridor we walk into Rowan and Hali kissing near the staircase. Hali is pinning Rowan against the wall, his arms wrapped around her, both their eyes closed, like they are the only two people here. Finn goes to clear his throat and I quickly

pull him into the side room.

"Shh! Do you know how long she's liked him? Give them a minute!" I whisper with haste. He looks at me and smiles.

"Playing Cupid?" he laughs.

"No. Just letting them have their fun." I smile. I look around the room I had pulled him into. Paintings cover the white marbled walls of men and women dressed in their finery. Huge banded crowns with intricate details of trees, flowers, fruits and landscapes sit upon the men's heads while a familiar twisted vine like band sat upon the females. "Are these all your ancestors?" I ask.

"Yes. This is the Kings office." My eyes widened with panic and I looked down at myself. My red bikini showing through the Prince's shirt, wet patches clinging to my skin. I tugged on the shirt trying to make it longer. This did not look good. Finn laughed. "The Fates are out." I let out a breath I didn't realise I was holding.

"The fates?" I ask, still struggling to tidy my attire.

"That is what we call our King and Queen. Collectively they are known as the fates."

He pulled my hand away from his shirt, coming towards me. "I like the outfit," he whispers in my ear, sending a shiver through me. He leans in close again, our lips almost touching, when the sound of footsteps echo through the hallway. He pulls away.

"I think they left. Come on. I'll take you to the mirror." My hands fly to my cheeks, trying to hide the flush.

As we enter the Seer's chamber, I wonder what my Father would have done here. I glanced at the papers on his desk. The last thing he wrote.

I'm being watched. I can feel something is coming for me, but their powerful magic hiding their face. Purple flames. They want my magic.

They want my daughter. She is the key to their end. The yellow canary marks the beginning. Nothing survives the purple flames wake. They will come for her. They will come for us all.

Images flash in through my mind. The purple flames from my dreams. My chest constricts in panic; it's all real.

"What's wrong?" Finn asks, looking down at the piece of paper. "Your dream? Your father has seen it too." His eyes wide with shock. I can't speak. I open my mouth and no words come out.

"Come on I will take you home. You need to rest," he says, taking the paper from my hands.

"He was taken." I said, a tear escaping. "I knew he wouldn't just leave us." Finn embraced me in a hug. His warmth enveloping me. I bury my face in his strong chest and a feeling of calmness takes over. We stay there, wrapped in each other unable to pull away, like something is binding us together, pulling us together, like magnets.

"I should go home." I say into him. He pulls away slowly. I let go and walk towards the mirror.

"I should speak with your grandmother and tell her what has happened," he says. I put my hand on his chest stopping him. He was still shirtless.

"I don't think your dressed appropriately." I say taking in his muscular chest. He looks down.

"We are quite the sight," he says staring at me once more.

"It's fine. I'll talk to her. Thank you for saving me," I smile, pulling my hand from his chest. I press my hand against the mirror. It buzzed with life.

"Thea." He says, I turn to look at him and he is lost for words. "Be careful until I next see you. I can't save you if I'm not there," he smiles.

"I'll try." I smile and I push through the mirror.

Chapter 6

I woke with a jump, a scream rumbling deep in my throat, breathing to ease the denseness in my chest. In and out. In and out. The nightmare is getting worse. The same sequence of events that feel more and more real as days go on. My arm still hurting even after I wake. A splitting headache clouding my thoughts. I move to the end of the bed, Toby grumbles as I push the covers away, but he falls back to sleep quickly.

I wonder if Dad had seen more of my vision. Maybe something different. I head over the mirror and place my hand on the glass. The ripple of magic spreads across the mirror showing me the Seers Tower. My father's room. I rub my eyes. Finn was asleep leaning over the desk. Should I wake him? That can't be comfortable, he probably has the fluffiest bed with the softest pillows. Why was he here?
I step through the mirror. And gently tap him on the shoulder.

"Finn." I whisper, trying not to wake anyone else up. "Finn." I whisper a little louder. He shakes awake, pulling away. He pries his tired eyes open.

"Thea? What are you doing here?" he says sleepily. "Are you alright?"

"I had another nightmare and couldn't get back to sleep. I wanted to search for clues," I whisper. "If you don't mind that is. I just realised this may count as breaking and entering," I spiral.

"No, it's fine." He yawns.

"What are you doing sleeping here?" I ask. His eyes opened wide at the question.

"Well, you just looked so sad earlier. I wanted to take a look at your Dad's things myself, to see if there was anything more the guards had missed." He stacks the pieces of paper neatly on the table. I smile internally, a warm feeling spreading through my chest.

"Thank you, but you look really tired. I think you should go to bed. That desk doesn't look the comfiest." I gesture to the mark on his face he had acquired from sleeping on a hard surface. He rubbed his cheeks, looking more awake he looks me up and down.

"That's what you wear to bed?" he smiles.

Oh shit! I hadn't thought about it. I was wearing an oversized jersey that came down to mid-thigh with long sleeves. Nothing further down.

"Better than nothing I suppose?" I say awkwardly, tugging it down. He smiles again.

"I like it. I would have liked it more if you had worn my shirt." He laughed. His eyes deep and green, like soft meadow grass I want to fall into. I must admit I had thought about it, but had decided against it, an internal battle that I couldn't win.

"Finn. You're getting married. I can't let this happen. I don't want to be the one left behind. I really like you already and this is just going to make it painful." I gesture to the both of us. He stands up, pulling me into his arms.

"I'm going to stop it. Something is going on. The fact the Princess is sending Sea hags after you and knows where you are, she must have spies. How she knows about us, I don't know." He rubs my arms. "I don't want to be with her. Not even politically. I want you." His voice turns into a whisper, his hand rising to stroke my cheek.

"What if you can't stop it? We hardly know each other. What if your dreams are trying to fool you?"

"I knew it when we kissed. You're the only one I will ever want." He leans down to kiss me. Desperation, in the air, like it was something he needed. I pushed away.

"I just can't. Until the wedding is off. I ... I don't want to make this worse for you. I don't want to get hurt." I whisper, pain in my voice.

He steps away. "I'm sorry." He reaches his hand out to me and then just drops it back down to his side. His eyes clouded with turmoil. "Goodnight Thea." He looks away and heads for the door, closing it firmly behind him.

I let out a little sob, stopping myself quickly. I can't do this to myself. I can't do this to him. If we go any further and the wedding still happens? It would break me. I barely know the guy, but I can feel him take root deep in my soul, if he were to be taken away, my heart wouldn't survive.
I pull myself together and look around the cold tower. The fire was lit, illuminating the room in the orange light. I started to flick through the dusty papers on the desk. Apart from the one I read earlier, most were notes from previous visions and some looked like visions he was trying to seek. Nothing of use to me though.
 I lean back in the chair and place my hands over my eyes. There must be something here. Exhaustion taking over, I yawn and head back to the mirror, a flapping noise accompanying me. A piece of paper had attached itself to my foot. I pull it off gently and place it back on the table, immediately double taking. This could be something. Purple flames drawn around the edge of a symbol. An intricate design of weaving thorny vines, similar to a Celtic rune. This has got to be something. I just need to find out what. I will show Finn tomorrow. I turn once again and slip through the mirror, crashing onto my bed as soon as I enter my room.

The hall was filled with white flowers. Two large sections of row upon row of seats, with an aisle through the middle. White petals falling from the sky, like snowflakes. I see Hali and I wave, her gaze going straight through me. Finn is stood at the altar, dressed in his royal blue suit. His hair tidied, but his eyes were vacant. The procession starts, a woman wearing a black wedding dress and thick black veil enters at the end of the room. The bottom of her dress covered in the purple runes. This can't be happening. I run to Finn, but he can't see me. He's not even moving, like a statue. The Bride is getting closer, the room darkening with every step that she takes.

"Please, no." I say covering my mouth in shock. The bride looks at me, smile illuminated through her dark veil. The petals turned black and the flowers began to wilt. The smell of rot filling my nostrils.

"They are mine now." She growls, laughing at her victory. I run to Hali, shaking her.

"Please Hali, you have to help me stop this. Hali please see me, wake up." Her eyes fixed ahead. "Please." I cry, shaking her, but she can't escape the trance.

"You see. You are not the key to the end. I am more powerful than you will ever be. Your friends are gone," she growls, her eyes turning back to Finn. He turns, smiling at her. His eyes though. They're clouded. She holds up her hand towards me.

"Time to go, Thea," she says, sending a black cloud towards me. The smell of death. I do the only thing I can do. I scream.

I shoot up in bed. Two in one night. Fantastic.

"Are you okay dear?" Gran shouts from the floor below.

"Yeah, just another nightmare." I shout, rubbing my face to calm myself.

"I heard you shout for help," she says. Did I shout?

"No, it's okay. It was just the dream," I reply. I hear her climb the stairs towards me. She turns and sits on the top step.

"Same fire?" she asks.

"No, a wedding actually. And a bridezilla." She laughs a little. She stands and sits on the edge of the bed. Taking my hand.

"Let me see." She closes her eyes, her brow furrows with concentration. "That's not good. That's the Prince's wedding, that I don't think he is present for." She shakes her head. "Has he met his Bride yet?"

"No." I look down at the bed.

"There may be something I can teach you that will help," she says finger on forehead thinking. "Right, how did your father do it?" she mumbles to herself.

"Do what?"

"Well, your father was a dream weaver. He can make people dream what he wants them to see. This power also let him communicate with others, sending messages to their mind."

"Telepathy?" I ask shocked. "How?"

"Right." She straightens on the bed. "Hold my hands and close your eyes. Now think of something you want to tell me. Anything. Something I wouldn't know already. Now imagine that message following through you. Down your arms, through your hands and into mine. Then up into my mind. Like how you let me see your dreams."

I think. *'I was the one who smashed the vase.'* Dad took the blame for that but it's something she might not know. That's a safe thing to tell her. It's not like I'm going to tell her about Finn.

I imagine the message moving, like a paper aeroplane, soaring down my arms and up into my grandmother's mind.

"You didn't?!" she said smacking my wrist.

"At least we know it worked. I'm sorry, I know Dad took the blame, but I was 10 and my mum would have killed me."

"What?" she said, confused.

"The vase you gave Mum and Dad for their wedding anniversary. I broke it."

"That's not what you just said. You said you and Finn kissed." I looked at her shocked.

"That was not the message I sent." The word ERROR flashing through my head as if I were sending emails.

"My fault, I forgot to tell you to clear your mind. You must only think of the message. If you don't, whatever is in your mind will go." She wafted her hands in the air like a butterfly taking flight. "It worked anyway, so next step. We won't hold hands, but the message will fly from your mind to mine, like it's on a piece of string." She ties the imaginary string to her head.

I think hard.
'Only the vase. Only the vase. Only the Vase'. Shooting the paper aeroplane straight into her mind.

"It was a bit jumbled, but that is to be expected. I did hear vase, so that's good. With practice, you will be able to send them to whoever you want, wherever you are." She smiled.

"Instant messages, without the monthly plan." I said as if I were an advert.

"Quite." She laughed.

"Now, this kiss. Seems like the Prince is a little unsure he wants to get married. Be careful. I don't want you getting hurt and from the looks of that dream, something bad is coming." She shuddered. "I will make you a tea to help with the lack of sleep. I will also start on a potion to help you see through charms. This bride seems like she knows you. It will help you see past any spells she may have, covering her dark magic. It will take a little while though I need some more kelpie scales." My eyes bug out of my head as she headed down the stairs. "And best hurry, Len said Hali will be here in 5 minutes." I scramble out of bed and look at the time. 8:15am. Shit. I needed to hurry.

I run down the stairs, swinging my blazer over my shoulders as I go.

"Here you go." Grandma hands me the tea. I down it, slightly burning my lips.

"Thanks! See you later!" I say running out the front door.

Chapter 7

"I have THE best news," Hali say,s as I jump in the car. "I kissed Rowan yesterday. I thought, you know what? I'm just going to do it. So, I did," she said, proud of herself.

"I know, I saw everything." She blushed, turning a raspberry colour.

"How?" She's turning pinker by the minute.

"Finn was taking me back to the mirror. You were blocking the stairs. I didn't want to interrupt." I winked at her.

"Thanks girl!" she shouts, tapping me on the arm.

"So, what does it mean? He seemed to enjoy it as much as you did." I send her a cheeky grin.

"I don't know, but it felt so good," she said sinking into her seat. "Did you see those muscles at the beach? Woo!" she fanned herself with her hand. I couldn't contain my laughter. She was so happy her ears couldn't stop twitching. "Speaking of muscles. Being saved by the Prince?" she said in a high-pitched voice, Disney style and grinning manically. "Tell me everything."

I paused for a minute. "I can trust you right? Whatever is said between us stays there."

She looked at me faking shock. "I wouldn't expect anything less!" "Well, we kissed," I said, half scrunching my face preparing for the blast.

"OH MY NEPTUNE!" she screams hitting the wheel, accidentally hitting the horn at one point. "But he's getting married?" she gasps.

"I know. That's why I said I couldn't be with him," I said, a pang of pain hitting me in the chest.

"YOU told HIM? I swear, since you came to town, my gossip gills are through the roof. Why does he like you so much? No offence, but he hardly knows you," she asks confused.

"Again, sworn to secrecy. I've been having this vision dream about him since before we met. That's why I acted weird when I met him." Her mouth gaps open. "And he's been dreaming of me too." Hali jumps in her seat, dancing side to side and a Cheshire grin spread over her face.

"So, what are you going to do?" she asks, biting her fingernails.

"Hope, I guess. I don't want him to get married. He doesn't even want to marry her, but I can't stand in his way," I shrug, trying to act casual but feeling like I've been shot.

"Oh, guppy," she says, pulling into the school car park. "Let's hug it out." She parks the car and reaches over the centre console. "In case you didn't already know, I'm team Fae," she whispers in my ear.

"Thanks Hali. I look out of the window. Looks like a certain other Prince Charming is waiting for you." I point over her shoulder. Rowan is leaning against a red brick wall, smiling at us.

"Eep!" the noise escapes her.

"Quick, go see him," I urge, nudging her out of the car.
She grins widely, hugging me once more. She waves her hand over her face, trying to gain composure, and gets out the car casually.

I get out and watch her walk over to him. He takes a hand from behind is back and looks around. Seeing the coast clear, a single flower appears in his hand. Within a moment, she dives on him, kissing him, nearly taking him off his feet.

"So much for composure," I laughed.

"Composure?" I hear Finn behind me, heart hits its cage like a meteor. I point casually at the couple. "Well, they are eager." He smiles.

"I think it's cute. They make a great couple." I nod approvingly.

"They are practically a different species." He laughs. I dart him a look.

"The heart wants what the heart wants." He looks down, avoiding my gaze.

"I just came to give you this." He hands me a blue envelope with gold trim. Surely not a wedding invitation?

"Are these the royal colours?" I say, images of the suit flashing from my dream.

"Yes," he smiles, dropping it when seeing my face. "What?" he asks. The bell ringing in the background.

"It's nothing," I smile. I don't want him to think I'm creating problems, so he doesn't get married. He is already trying to stop it. I open the envelope slowly, my heart clenching expecting the worst, to see it is an invite to the Summer Solstice ball this Saturday. I let out a big breath, I didn't realise I was holding. Finn raises a quizzical eyebrow at me. "Thank you for this." I smile as he nods briefly in response.

We head into the school. As we pass Hali and Rowan, I tug on her arm. "Class," I whisper. She pulls away from his embrace slightly dazed. Finn pulls Rowan in the opposite direction. "See you later Rowan." I shout. She smiles and waves at him, he returns a blown kiss.

"Here's a question. Why the hell do you go to school? You're magical beings going to a school that has no idea you even exist."

Her gaze finally snaps back. "You could literally go home and make out all day," I laugh.

"Well, Finn, the Prince," she starts. I roll my eyes.

"Of course," waving my hand for her to continue.
"He wanted to go," she said, "to become a good King I need to know the neighbours." She mimics him, holding her arms out like she has muscles.

"So why do you go?" I ask.

"Well, we were already friends. Finn, Rowan, Eva and I, so we just went with him. It's cool to understand another culture and learn their history." She smiled.

"So, like foreign exchange. Without the exchange." I smiled.

"We took you in, didn't we?" she joked.

"Touché. I suppose I am only half Fae. You have to start somewhere." I laughed. "Want to hear a new skill I learned?"

"Sure!" she smiled. We sat down at our desks and I took her hand.

'Rowan smudged your lipstick,' I thought, send the message through me to her. Her eyes went wide in horror. Digging through her bag for a mirror.

"You let me walk through the school like this?" she whispered, annoyance in her voice.

"I wanted to show you my new skills." I shrugged.

"I must admit that was very cool. We can have a secret conversation. Well, with you doing all the talking."

"Well, that's unusual," I say sarcastically, flashing her my raised eyebrows.

"Whatever."

"So, what happened to your composure when you saw Rowan?"

bobbing my eyebrows up and down.

"That flower. It pushed all the composure of the table. He's just so god damn cute!" she says through gritted teeth. I couldn't help but laugh and feel a hint of envy.

As the lunch bell rang, my eyes jittered open. Dozing in Math, how cliché of me. Hali scrambled her books into her bag.

"Well, look who's back in the land of the living?" she laughed. "Your head has been lolling for the last half an hour." She smiled.

"It's hard to get any decent sleep these days," I yawned.

"How come?"

"The dreams that I have, well more like nightmares. It used to be just the one with purple flames and Finn running to me. Last night was a new one. It was Finn's wedding. It was bad."

"OOOh, do tell?" she says, throwing her bag over her shoulder. I wonder for a moment if I should.

"Well it was Finn's wedding. It was bad. You both were like Zombies." Her eyes widened.

"Can you show me?" she said holding out her hand. I took her hand. she closes her, her eyebrows raising up and down.
"Have you shown this to Finn?" she says slowly letting go of my hand.

"Well no. I don't want him to think I'm being that girl."

"Oh yeah that girl. The one who has vision of a wedding that potentially ends in her death. The one he was planning on backing out of with the crazy ass bride. Oh yeah, and the guests all in a trance. We don't want to be that girl." she said sarcastically.

"So, you think I should show him?"

"DUH! It's bad. that is true, he needs to be prepared." She says, weaving a path through the crowded corridor. We get to the cafeteria and sit down at the table. The smell of cookies, wafting through the air, tingling my taste buds. Hali squeezes between Rose and Rowan.

"Thank God it is the last day tomorrow. And then we have the Ball this Saturday! So exciting." Hali dances in her seat.

"So, what is the Ball for?" I ask.

"The annual Summer Solstice Ball. It is when the Fates bring in the summer season in with the great pollination."

"Pollination?"
"Why do you care?" Eva bites.

"I was just wondering what to expect that's all."

"You got an invite?" Rose scowled.

"Yeah, I gave her the invite today," Finn said, approaching the table. Rose slides next to me, filling the opening and creating a lovely space next to her. "Why wouldn't she get an invite?"

"Oh, I just thought the invites had already been sent out. I thought your mother might not appreciate a late entry." She smiled, extremely falsely. "I didn't mean anything by it." batting her eyes with all the vulnerability of a tiger.

"How about I worry about my mother? What is one more, added on to 500?" he smiled at me, my eyes bug out of my head.

"Do you know what you are going to wear?" Rose smiles, as if making girl talk.

"What am I supposed to wear?" Eva and Rose giggle to themselves. I flick around the food on my plate. Spaghetti Bolognese but the meat is still undecided.

"It's the most coveted event in the calendar." Eva laughs. "Not that, that's for sure." She says pointing to my uniform. They erupt in laughter. Honestly the joke was lost on me. She was wearing the same thing.

"I don't have my dress either," Hali pipes in, finally able to pull her attention from Rowan.

"Well I can fix that. How about you two come over tomorrow evening to get fitted? The Royal dressmaker can see that you both are wearing something suitable," Finn winks at me. Eva and Rose fall silent, looking from me to him.

"Definitely!" Hali replies immediately. "We will be the best-looking girls at the ball! We will be able to snag you a man if we are lucky." She gives me an evil grin. Finn's jaw tightens, his eyebrows furrow and anger clouding his eyes. That comment hit true and she relishes in his expression. I could see the excitement on her face. She will be retelling me about this later.

"Snagging men isn't really high on my to do list at the minute," I shrug, "but I can definitely go for the dressing up and the dancing." I smile, catching Finn's face relaxing out of the corner of my eye. I don't want to make him jealous. His decision is already hard, and I've never been that kind of girl. Hali rolls her eyes dramatically at me.

"Anyway, do you want to go with me to the ball?" Rowan says turning to Hali. Her eyes lit up like a Christmas tree. I could feel her excitement radiating across the table, smacking me in the face, I could smell it too. Like cherry pie. Which is a little weird.

"Like as a date?" she asked, vibrating. He nodded in response and she leaped onto him, knocking him onto the ground, squealing. The cafeteria erupted in laughter, but she didn't care. She was so happy.
As I walk through the front door to my Grandmother's house, the usually smell of rosemary and lavender fill my senses.

"Thea, come in to the kitchen. It's time for a lesson," she says, popping her head so she could see me coming down the hallway.

"What lesson are we having?" I asked placing my bag down on the kitchen table and taking a seat.

"I'm going to teach you control. Then potions." She places her cup and saucer down on the oak table.

"I can control the dreams?"

"With practice, but I'm talking about bringing your gift forward, calling to it."

"What do you mean?"

"Let's try it. You'll understand. I want you to close your eyes. Clear your mind. Focus. We will start easy. Think of your mother. What her uniform looks like. Her hair." Her voice soft, calming me. I did I was told but first there was nothing. Just the image of my mother, her long dark hair swept back into a bun. I dug deeper. Pulling at my mind. It felt like static. As if tuning an old TV a picture started to come into view.

"She's here," I said as the handle turned on the door.

"Good job." Gran whispered. Gripping my hand. "We will try again later. We can try some potions now, while we make dinner."

"Thea! How was school?" my mother said placing her handbag on the sideboard and taking off her jacket.
"Fine, not much happening seeing as it is the last day tomorrow." I smiled.

"How are your friends? It feels like I've barely seen you this week with all your gallivanting," she joked.

"They're good. I will be going over to Hali's tomorrow and Saturday, if that's alright?"

"Of course! What are the names of your other friends?" she asks while pouring herself a cup of tea.

"Rowan and Finn, there are two girls called Eva and Rose as well but I'm not sure on those two. I don't think they like me."

"Why wouldn't they like you?" her brow furrowing.

"No reason I can think of. I think it's probably because I'm new there or something." I notice my grandma side eyeing me from the chopping board.

"Well they will come around I suppose. I'm just going to change out of my uniform," she says, heading for the stairs.

"Right Thea. This potion is probably the most important. Healing." Taking the jars of the shelves. "It can be made into a drinkable or a paste, depending on what kind of ailment it is. First, we will make a drinkable one. A smidge of rosemary, turmeric…" she lists off the ingredients handing me the pots one at a time. I throw them in the mortar grinding them down as I go. "Right. Now we boil them in water."

I bring it over the already warmed pan and pour them in slowly. "The most potent healing potions contain dragon tears. But they are very hard to come by."

"Because of the lack of dragons?" I laughed.

"No dear, because dragons rarely cry," she said shaking her head. I stare dumbfounded.

"You have a lot to learn," she laughs. "Now like last time, you must put a little magic into it." I stirred the potion. A green plume of smoke shot out the top, forming a tree, before dissipating in the air. "Good job. This should make about three potions. I want you to keep one on you at all times. You never know when you could run into trouble." Grandma started pouring the mixture into little vials and handed me one. She then went over to the spice rack and pulled. I flinched, waiting for the spices to come tumbling down, but instead a cupboard opened. Inside was filled with vials of all different potions, labels on each shelf to distinguish what they all were. *Truth potion, sleeping draft, total knock out-* that name made me laugh. *Memory potion, memory eraser, power be gone, transporter.*

"What is 'Lion and Lamb'?" I asked intrigued.

"Where you can make something little, big, or big, little. Very interesting potion that one. Not many use it, that's why it is collecting dust." She turns to me. "I thought I had best show you this cupboard. I always keep it stocked. You are welcome to use anything at any time, but please be careful. If your dreams are anything to go by, something terrible is coming." She took a sip of her tea. "Now seeing as your mother still isn't down, I want you to look for someone else. Please tell me where Finn is." I dart her a look.

"I am not spying on him." I said shaking my head.

"Dear, it is not spying. It is a lesson. Only a quick peak to practice then we will move on." I sit down in the table, closing my eyes, letting the static cloud fill my mind while I tune in on Finn. His green eyes, dark onyx hair, chiselled jaw line. His face comes into view. The background clears to show his bedroom.

"He's at the castle. He's looking through his desk. He feels mad about something." I notice his drawing of me is pinned to the wall above. I pull away from the vision. "I don't want to watch anymore. I feel like I'm invading his privacy."

"I understand, but it is all good progress. The closer you are to the person, the easier it is." She grinned.

"You tricked me." I wafted the tea towel at her.

"I may not have the gift of sight, but there are other means to get the information I want," she laughs.

"Now a harder one. Tell me where the Unseelie Princess is." She said a wave of seriousness coming over her face.

"How?"

"Use your dream. What you remember about her. What she sounded like. Use all these to narrow your sights on her." she said sipping at her tea. It must be cold by now.

"I'll try." I concentrated on the dream, letting the static fill my mind. The static grew. The buzzing noise filling my ears. A tiny glimpse of the princess comes into view.

"No more." Grandma said, breaking the connection.

"I was almost there." I said flicking open my eyes. I felt tears roll down my cheeks.

"She has a barrier charm on her." she hands me a tissue.
"How do you know?"

"Your tears are blood. If you fought through much longer you might have seen her, but you might have scrambles your brain also." I wiped my eyes seeing the blood disperse within the tissue. "She knew this would happen. Her defences are up." She shook her head. "Your father would be proud of your progress. You are learning quickly." She smiled and rubbed my hand.

"I went to his office last night. The Seers tower. I think I might have found something." Her eyes lit up.

"What?" she said as the sound of my mother's feet coming down the stairs echoed through the hall.

"I think he saw this coming. He saw my visions too," I said rooting around in my school bag and pulling out the drawing.

"The purple flames." She said, her eyes wide with shock, she hands it back for me to hide.

"I'm sorry that took so long. My boss called; she can get a little chatty. So, what shall I make for dinner?"

"Anything you like Mum. Your pick."

Chapter 8

No dreams came. The sound of tapping on my window woke me. I rubbed my eyes to clear my vision. Len.

"Okay, I'm up," I shout. I look at the alarm clock on my dresser. Seven thirty. Not too shabby. I had a shower, got dressed and headed downstairs. Grandma was sat at the kitchen table, Len on the work top.

"I see you send your minions to wake me now." She laughed into her teacup.

"Len was concerned for your lateness." She smiled, placing a teacup in from of me and pouring the tea. "Now, how was your sleep?"

"Uneventful. No dreams to report." Her gaze softened.

"I'm glad to hear that. Now, this picture you showed me yesterday. May I see it again?" I took out the picture and handed it over, trying not to scrunch it. "As I had thought. This is the symbol of the Unseelie," she said, pointing to the symbol in the flames.

"You think the Unseelie Princess is behind the burning?"

She nodded. "I fear so. We need more information. And you need to be able to protect yourself."

I sipped my tea.
"Dad made me take all those kickboxing and self-defence classes back in Chester. I can take care of myself." She shook her head.

"If your dreams are correct, you might not be able to get out without a fight. A real fight," she said, rising from her chair. "Come with me." I followed her to her bedroom. She opened up her wardrobe and parted the clothes, revealing a small hidden door. She unlatched the small hook and pushed the door open hard, uncovering a range of weapons. A crossbow, a bow, a sword and a set of daggers.

"Grandma! What the hell?" I screeched, my eyes bulging.

"These were my past time when we lived in the Seelie Realm," she said, stroking one of the blades.

"I thought you said you were a healer?"

"I was, primarily, but I loved a good battle. As the royal healer, I was required to go to any battles and in my time, there were a few. To go to a battlefield and not know how to fight is beyond stupid. I want you to learn. The classes your dad made you attend are good, if you're in that situation, but in this case, you will need this," she says, handing me the sword, my arm dropping from the weight.

"I didn't realise you were a bad ass!"

"I will make some calls. Your friend Rowan has been training to be in the Royal Guard. Maybe you could ask him for a lesson this evening?"
"I'm going to the palace tonight. Finn has said he will get the dressmaker to make mine and Hali's dress for the ball." A grin spread across her face as I spoke his name.

"Sounds lovely. Maybe you could get a lesson at the castle from the Prince himself?" she smiled.

"Maybe. I don't think I have it in me to kill anyone. It's crazy." I pass her back her sword.

"Dear, it's about knowing how to protect yourself if you need to, not about killing people. The Unseelie are known for their ruthlessness. I don't want you to be unprepared," she says, taking my hand and squeezing it. "The Summer Ball is a grand event. I will be there also." Changing the subject she pulled a large silver gown out of her hidden room.

"It's beautiful. You got invited as well?"

"Of course. I would never miss it," she smiled. "I am looking forward to seeing what you choose to wear."

"I don't really have a clue."

"I'd go with red. It always looked good on you." She smiled, twirling my hair in her fingers.

"Red it is," I replied and the familiar honk sounded, telling me Hali was outside.

"I am so excited about our dresses tonight," she said as soon as I got into the car. "I have drawn up some ideas that came to me last night." She handed me a book out of her bag and pulled away from the house.

"These are amazing." Two dresses on either side of the page, she had named each page to show who the dress was for. Hali's was blue, with a sparkly grey tulle layered over it. the neckline was a plunging one and there were tied ribbons at the shoulders. "You're going to look amazing in this." I said when I turned to look at mine. It was a shiny material, silk maybe? With a cowl neckline and a split up the leg and hugged waist then flowed out into the skirt. She hadn't decided on a colour.

"Do you like it? I thought you might want to choose the colour." She searched my face for clues.

"I love it! I was thinking a red. I didn't know you could draw," I smile shoving her a little.

"Great idea, very femme fatale," she smiles, pouting her lips at me.

"Of course." I respond with my best smoulder. "Thank you this are amazing."

"It's no biggie. I had mine already down, but then last night I thought of you and your 'situation' and I thought, I am going to make you the sexiest bitch there." She nodded, approvingly.

"Thank you." I lean over and give her a car hug. An idea hit me. "Hey, do you know how to fight?" she took a little double take. "Why?" she asked bemused.

"Well my Grandma is worried something is coming. She wants me to be ready to protect myself."

"If she said it then it must be true. I trust that woman more than myself. Yes, I can fight. More far away stuff than up close. I'm good with a bow and throwing daggers. We could ask Finn about using the armoury at the castle," she says eyes ablaze.

"You think he would let us?"

"He would most probably let you do anything." She winks at me. "But yes, he loves a good fight. He would want to help. We all know you could do with it."

"Thanks, I guess." We pulled into the car park, Rowan running to the car as soon as he saw us, Finn walking behind him.

"Someone has it bad." I gestured to him.

"Good. Because so do I," she sighs, pulling up the handbrake. Rowan opens her door. Finn comes around to my side, but I open it before he gets there.

"I was going to get that," he smiles.

"I'm an independent woman. I can get my own door," I joked.
"But it sure is nice having it done for me," Hali says kissing Rowan's cheek. "Hey Finn, Thea wants to learn to fight. Can we use your armoury after the dress fitting?"

"Sure, but why?" he said, looking at me puzzled.

"Althea said she thinks something bad is coming. She wants Thea to be ready for fight. After her dream about your wedding and all," she shrugged. I flash her a killer gaze. I hadn't told him yet.

"What dream?" his eyes filled with worry.

"Oops. She can show you. Bye." She turns, waving and walking away dragging Rowan behind her.

"I'm sorry I didn't tell you yesterday."

"Can I see?" he asked, holding out his hand. I take it and he closes his eyes. he grimaces as the dream ends and he opens those gorgeous eyes back up. "This is bad." He rakes his fingers through his hair. "What did your Grandma say?"

"She's worried. We were practicing last night, and she asked me to look for my mother, that was easy, then you, which was also easy, and then the Princess. I couldn't really see anything and then my eyes bled."

"A barrier charm. Are you okay?" he asked, pulling my chin up so he could look at me. It sends a pleasant shiver down my body, tingling my senses, the smell of him making me feel a little dizzy.
"I'm fine. She pulled me out before it got bad." Trying to keep myself, from looking into his gorgeous eyes, I pull away a little. "There is one more thing. I found this in the Seers tower that night." I took out the drawing from my bag. His eyes opened wide with shock. "She said that's the symbol of the Unseelie, which you probably know already, but the purple flames?"

"Too much to be a coincidence." I nodded in agreement. "I must bring this to the King and Queen. This will make them reconsider." The bell sounds but he runs opposite direction.

"Aren't you coming?" I shouted after him.

"I have more pressing matters," he shouts back, waving the picture in the air.

"Alright everyone! Time for your presentation on Welsh Folklore! I have put all the groups into this bowl and will pull them out to see who will go first." She roots around in the fishbowl of names and finally lands on one. "The tale of King Arthur. Thea and Hali are you ready?"

Of course, we would be first. We gather our notes and head to the front.

"Your 2 minutes starts now." She turns the egg timer.

"King Arthur was a legendary King of Britain, the one true King, though the history around his reign is shrouded in mystery. Firstly, was he even the King at all? Where was Camelot? Legends and folklore of King Arthur's reign is filled with magic from Merlin, the wizard and wiseman who helped Arthur Pendragon to dragons, Druids and Morgana, the evil witch you waged war against him. His magical sword, Excalibur, is said to be from Bosherston here in Pembrokeshire." I looked over to Hali to carry on.

"He was known for his ruling being a fair and just one. He brought about the round table for his knights, so everyone was of equal status. One of the most well-known stories of Arthur revolves around the love triangle between himself, Guinevere his wife, and one of his Knights, Lancelot. This led to the quest of the holy grail and his death"

"Thank you for listening," we said together.

"Lovely girls. 1:48 minutes. Well done," Miss Russell clapped.

"Seeing as how it only took us 5 minutes to Google," Hali whispered.

"Shhh!" I laughed. I had only been here a week!

The bell finally rang for the end of the day. The classroom erupts in cheers as they swarm for the door.

"Please remember your summer reading! Have a great summer!" she shouts as we head out the classroom.

"Thea! Hali!" Finn shouts, weaving through the crowd to get to us.

"How did talking to your parents go?" I ask, trying not to sound concerned.

"They were out and apparently won't be back until tomorrow morning before the ball," he shrugged. "I was thinking though, if you guys are coming over anyway why don't you guys stay and get ready for the Ball at the castle? Rowan has said he will help us later at the armoury."

Before I can say a word, Hali shouts "Sure! We would love to. I will just take Thea home to get her stuff." She pulls me away quickly towards the car.

"Just come through the mirror!" he shouts behind us.

"Why were you going to say no?" she whisper-shouts at me.

"It's a little weird right?"

"No! We always stay there! Plus, how are you ever going to win unless you put yourself out there?" she prods me in the shoulder.

"I don't want to win. I want him to do what he feels is right. He has more at stake." She rolls her eyes and her head, just to show how idiotic she thought I was.

"There is nothing more important. I am not going to stand by and let him marry someone he doesn't even know." She scowls. "He has been my friend since before I can remember. Me, Him and Rowan. He closed off when this wedding was announced. He has never wanted it and I won't let it happen." She walks faster, storming towards her car.

"Okay, okay. He just seems so confused. I just don't want to add to the burden," I shout across the car roof before sliding in.

"I understand what your trying to say but you're wrong. He needs us to be there for him. Not push him away."

"Okay I'm sorry." I put a hand on her shoulder. "I do have an idea for tonight. Have you ever watched Pretty Woman?" I smiled.

"Duh. I love movies. Why?" she asked.

"Can we watch movies at the castle? Finn hasn't seen it."

"Well we could bring a laptop and a DVD if you have one. That should work. There isn't any electricity in the castle, unless you count the romantic sparks." I gave the shut-up look.

"We can have a movie night after our busy day."

"That sounds nice. Get his frustration out with the fighting then a chilled night. I like that idea. Plus, I can cuddle," she started dancing, "because I have a guy now."

"Yeah, yeah. Just focus on you driving. I want to get home in one piece."

"Good day dear?" Grandma asked as we approached the house.

"Yeah. We're going to the palace now and we're staying over, if that's alright."

"Oh, are we now?" she said with a smile. "I'll tell your mother you are at Hali's," she winked.

"Thanks Althea. I will make sure she stays out of trouble." Hali winked back, "and teach her a few of my moves." She slices the air with a flat palm.

"Good! Now you had best head off! If you are going through the mirror, make sure you are holding hands. Because of the charm we put on it, no one will be able to step through apart from our bloodline. Now get going. I will see you tomorrow at the ball."

"Would you like to see the dresses I drew?" Hali says digging through her bag.

"No dear. I prefer surprises!" she smiled, and shooed us into the house.

In my bedroom I start to pile the things into a holdall. I grab my laptop, placing it in gently and look through my draws for pjs.

"Can you look on that shelf for 'Pretty Woman?' It should be there," I ask, pointing to the shelf under the window, while grabbing some clothes to change into. Some leggings, a sports bra and a t-shirt. Ready for battle, I suppose.

"Got it!" she said placing it into my bag. "You are not bringing these pjs are you?" she said pointing to an oversized t-shirt and bottoms.

"Why not?"

"You at least want to look presentable, for Neptune's sake." She said digging through my drawers again. "How about this?" she pulled out a black vest and shorts.

"I am not wearing those shorts in a Palace." Shaking my head.

"Fine wear this top and those bottoms," she starts shoving in the top before I can argue.

"Will I need to come back here for a shower in the morning?"

"Funny enough, they have wash facilities at the palace. Good ones too." I nodded and took the toiletry bag off the shelf and went to fill it up. After a minute or two we were ready to step through the portal. I held out my hand for her to take.

"How come you put a charm on it?"

"I woke up one night and someone was watching me through it and then they had been in my room. I think it might have been Finn, but I didn't want to say. My Gran insisted on the charm." I shrugged.

"He has it bad for you!" she laughed.

"Come on!" I shove her, then pull her through the mirror.

"Great! You're here!" Finn says as we enter the Seers Tower.

"Have you been waiting for us?" I ask.

"Or trying to spy?" Hali laughs, and I prod her in the shoulder.

"What?"

"You have been spying on Thea, like a stalker. Sneaking into her room." She laughed even harder. I feel my cheeks flush with colour.

"What?" he asks again, more concerned.

"Look, it's not a big deal, she saw you." Hali laughs playfully shoving him. His face tenses and he closes his eyes tightly.

"If someone was spying on you, it wasn't me." he says simmering. "Someone was in your room?" anger spilling from him. "When?" he steps forwards and reaches for the mirror, but its blocked. I place my hand on his chest. His anger and concern spreads through me.

"A couple of days ago. There's a spell on it now so only I can go in and out of it. It really wasn't you?" He shakes his head.

"Then who in Neptune's name has been watching you?" Hali asks, her eyes wide.

"Let's not get into this now. The charm is on the mirror. No one can get into my room. We have a lot to do so let's go." I gently shove them both from the room. They looked at each other concerned. "Please. Can we drop it for now?" the calmness in my voice shaking slightly. It was more of a hope thinking it was Finn, but now it seems more sinister. A shiver travels up my spine.

"Okay." Hali finally spoke. "Take us to the Royal Dressmaker. I have our orders." She smiled wearily at me and then Finn. He turned and headed for the door, without a word, leading us to his sitting room.

"She's waiting for you in there," he said, showing us in and then turning and walking down the hall with a huff.

"We'll meet you in the armoury in 20 minutes?" I ask. He stops, turns his head to the side and nods before carrying on.

Hali's attention was already on the dressmaker, her tall slender figure, with long blonde hair similar to Hali's. Soft features with long spindly fingers like individual wands.

"Could you make us these?" Hali said, handing her the drawings. The dressmaker nodded gracefully then beckoned Hali to the pedestal. She immediately began waving her hands around Hali, a silver cloud shrouding her. It was like watching the fairy godmother in Cinderella. It took everything in me not to sing the bippity song. After a few minutes the cloud disperses into a glitter, leaving behind Hali, in her gown. The colours were gorgeous, like the Caribbean Sea, the tulle overlaying the blue was a light grey, almost silver with sparkles of spirals imbedded into it.
"It's gorgeous." I say, hands on my cheeks.

"Yeah? Do you think Rowan will like it?" she asks sheepishly.

"If he doesn't, he will have me to deal with," I smile. She steps off the pedestal and does a quick spin in front of a mirror.

"Don't forget these." The dressmaker waved one hand over the other, revealing a pair of silver stilettos. "The good thing about magical heels is they never hurt. Especially like your human version. They are awful." She whispered as if it were a secret. Hali made a high-pitched squeal and took them excitedly, sitting in one of the chairs to tie up the straps.

"Right your turn," she said once more, gracefully pointing to the pedestal. The silver cloud grew around me as the dressmaker waved her arms once more, dancing with the magic in the air. My skin tingled as the magic swept over it and the smell of peonies filled the atmosphere. After a few minutes she lowered her hands and the cloud dispersed, leaving behind the scarlet dress. The cowl neckline modestly hid my cleavage, corset style top that flowed out at the waist into a gorgeous box pleat skirt. I was a little worried about the split, it came quite high up on my leg and I worried that with a swift turn, everything could be on show. As if reading my face, the dressmaker waved her hand over it, lowering it slightly. I smiled gratefully, shifting my dress from side to side, watching it shine in the light.

"You look amazing!" Hali said, almost as a whimper.

"Thanks to you both," I reply before stepping down. After the wave of her magical hand the dressmaker handed me a pair of red stilettos with straps that wrapped around my ankle.

"Thank you." I said taking them gingerly.

She curtsied. "If that will be all?" We both nodded and thanked her again as she went out the door and closed it behind her.

"Where did our normal clothes go?" I asked, looking around. Hali pointed to the small pile on the ornate table and I began to change back.

"We'll have to hide these," she said, hanging hers up. She takes mine and heads out of the room.

"Where did you put them?" I asked pulling back on my leggings.

"Where no one will find them." She smiled. "Now let's get you fighting fit. Follow me."

We head down the golden corridor and turn into what I think is the entrance hall where Finn brought me after the sea witch. A grand ornate staircase curves up on either side of the grand hall with a waterfall falling behind leading to a stream below. We head towards it and before taking a cold shower the crystal waterfall splits, allowing us passage behind. This hallway was stone. Not as bright as the rest of the castle. Blue and gold cloths draped the walls like an old Tudor castle. The double doors on the end were open and the sound of clashing metal echoed towards us.

"Seems they have started without us," Hali said, starting to jog. The room was huge. High ceilings with weapons on three walls, the other were multiple heavy wooden doors all leading out onto a garden. There was a space in the centre where Rowan and Finn were fighting. Sweat dripping off them as their sword clash and clanged together. Swinging at each other with such force I thought one was going to take the others head off. I gasped a few times; Hali laughed every time I did.

"We'll start off with me then." She heads over to the wall and grabs a bow, daggers and a quiver of arrows and nodded for me to follow her out into the garden.

"Put this quiver on your back," she says, placing the leather strap over my head and one shoulder. "Right. First of all, you can see the target, right?" she nods towards the suit of Armor stuffed with straw and about a thousand holes in it about 100 yards away. I nod in response. "Good. Glad you're not blind. Get a feel for the bow. Pull the string back a few times." She demonstrates then hands it over, and I copy what she does. "Good, now take an arrow out of the quiver and aim it." I gave her a suspicious look. "Just do it."
I raise the bow. "Now, you want to be able to see the length of the arrow. Elbow higher than your hand. Draw and release." I do as she says and miss completely.

"You need to aim it!" Rowan shouts. Him and Finn are headed towards us.

"She's hopeless." Hali laughs.

"It was my first go!"
"Prove me wrong then." She stands beside me arms folded. Great now I have an audience. I pull the bow once more. Taking homage

from Lara Croft, I pull the string to just behind my ear. I aim and release. The arrow flies through the air and skims the shoulder.

"Better." Hali nods. "but not good enough. Again." I send her a glare. I repeat the exercise once more, this time, hitting it in the shoulder. "Good! I knew you could do it! Now do it a hundred more times."

"Before that, how about some sword play?" Rowan says swinging the sword at his side, winking at Hali.

"You think you can handle me?" she says shoving him playfully in the chest before running back to the armoury. I shake my head.

"They are like kids," I laugh.

"Come on. I'll teach you." He takes the bow and drapes it over his shoulder and takes my hand. sending warmth and a tingling sensation all over my body. He pulls me back into the armoury.

"Take this." He hands me a stick from a bucket.

"A stick?"

"Better a stick than me slicing you with a sword."

"Who says you would get the chance?" I smile raising my wooden sword in front of me.
"Your sword is used for defence and attack. You block and strike." He moves the stick like a Jedi.

"Alright. Let's try, shall we?"

We start off slow knocking the swords against each other picking up speed with every strike. The clack of the wood satisfying my ear drums. He moves quickly tapping me in the ribs.

"Got too comfortable." He smiles. I see how it is. This time I go for a full-on attack. Swinging the sword left and right, upwards and downwards, again he taps me on the shoulder. He shrugs at his victory. I can feel the anger burning inside of me. I don't like

to lose, even if I am learning. I run at him, swinging the sword left and right like Legolas from Lord of the Rings. I catch him on the arm before he disarms me all together. My stick flies through the air with no possible way to recover it. He hands me another out of the bucket, a smug look on that gorgeous face. Not for long. Hopefully.
This time I take it a little slower. Watching and trying to anticipate his moves. He's pushing me backwards with every hit. I go to take one more step back and hit the wall with a thump. He closes the gap between us, raising the stick against my chest.

"You're getting it. The anger definitely helps. You see, I just don't like losing." He laughs, so close I can feel his words caress my skin. I can smell the sweat on his face, the droplets on his cheek. I could feel his muscles through his grey t-shirt. The warmth of his body against mine makes me shiver. He leans in closer, releasing the stick slightly. As he closes his eyes to kiss me, I whip the stick from my side and wrap it around his back, using it to turn us. I push him against the wall and push his own stick back against him. The look on his face slightly dumbfounded. I lean in close, my lips grazing his cheek and I whisper softly.

"Neither do I." and kiss him on the cheek.

"You see Finn! These girls man, they mess with your head!" I turn around to see Rowan, pinned on the mat by Hali kneeling around his head, smiling.

"You boys are big and strong. Us women have got to use something against you." She laughs, shimmying her legs down his body and kissing him before getting up. I turn back to Finn, his green eyes flicking all over my face, his lips slightly parted. His biceps stuck to his t-shirt, rippling.

"I don't think you would be able to do it again." He whispers. His breath is tickling my cheek. His eyes excited. His heat radiating against me. It takes everything in me not to kiss him.

"No, next time I'll take you down sooner." I whisper back. A little cocky, I know. He raises his eyebrows, his eyes smiling. I step away and drop the stick.

"Come on, Hali. I think the boys need to practice. You can show me where the showers are." I shout, my eyes fixed on Finn as she hooks my arm and we leave.

"That was hot," she whispered as we get into the corridor. "Best workout ever. How I didn't tear his clothes off I don't know." Hali laughed.

I let go of a breath I didn't realise I was holding. My heart was racing. "I could see that! How did you disarm him?"

"You want to talk about me? What happened to 'I don't want to add to the burden'?" she said in a mimicry voice that clearly wasn't my own. I shoved her playfully.

"He distracted me with his muscles." I admitted. "Where is the bathroom in this place?" I said looking around as we entered the main foyer.

"I'll take you." We head down the corridor towards Finn's room and she turns to the room on the right and opens the door. "You can bathe in here. I'll use the ensuite. Our room is this one here," she says pointing to the room she is heading into. I head to the Finn's sitting room, the one opposite, and pick up my bag. I hear the door click shut behind me.

"You really think this is over?" Finn is standing in front of the door. His t-shirt stuck to him with sweat, outlining his muscles. His eyes determined. He strides over to me, lifting me and wrapping my legs around his waist. Holding me against the wall. My breath catching in my throat. "Think you can get out of this one?" he whispers.

"I don't want to hurt you." His lips graze my neck. "And I don't think I want to." Grabbing his face and pushing my lips to his desperately. He presses up against me, his hands all over me, moving from my hips, over my back and up round to my chest. I put my fingers through his hair pulling him closer to me. the door clicks open behind and he drops me quickly, Finn turns his head to check who the intruder is.

"I'm sorry! I tried to sneak. Didn't mean to interrupt!" Rowan says crouching to the ground reaching for his bag. Finn scowls. "Carry on!" he says as he turns to leave the room.

"I had best get cleaned up. I stink." I say placing my hand on his muscular chest, pushing him away. "You too, you could use a clean shirt." I laugh, tugging his shirt away from his skin.

"I thought you like my shirt like this, you keep looking at it." he laughs. I laugh awkwardly and he pulls me into a hug. I nuzzle into his shoulder. "I will stop this wedding, and when I do, do you want to go on a date?" he asks, stroking my hair. I pull away and look into his eyes.

"Sounds perfect." I smile. "But for now, how about I get showered up and we watch 'Pretty Woman'?" I say, pointing to the laptop on the table.

"This sounds a lot like a human date." He smiles.

"With Rowan and Hali making out next to us, it might just be." I laugh and head for the door. He pulls back on my hand.
"I'm going to look after you. I'm not going to let anyone hurt you. If your visions are real..." he trails off, not knowing what to say.

"It's okay. We can look after each other." I kiss him on the cheek and head to the bathroom.

The bathroom was amazing. Gorgeous sandstone walls with a pebbled floor. The floor sloping into the bathtub like a pool. The water was constantly filled by the waterfall edges around the far wall. I strip down and dip my toe in to find it surprisingly warm. I submerge, the warmth of the water encapsulating me and my muscles relax on cue. I spend a little too long in there as a knock at the door, shakes me from my daze.

I rush to dry off and get dressed in my pjs. I return to Finn's sitting room to find Hali cuddled up to Rowan on the red sofa, they have covered with throw cushions, draping themselves with a grey soft blanket.

"The film is just starting." Hali must have set it up while I was bathing. Finn indicates to the space next to him. I sit down and he draped his arm around my shoulder, pulling me in close. I went to fight it but gave in, snuggling my head into his chest. Sleep taking me, almost as soon as I do.

I blink my eyes open, blurred vision obscuring my surroundings. A throbbing in my head that won't dissipate. The sound of a drip hitting a hard surface. The feel of a cold hard floor under my hands as I push myself up. I rub my eyes. A wooden door and 4 stone walls. Bars cover the window. A cell? I scramble to my feet, standing on my tip toes to see out the window. Darkness covers the land. The smell of rotten food, dead fish and sour milk fills my nostrils till I gag. Where am I? I head to the small barred window in the door.

"Is anyone there?" I shout. No one answers.

I wake with a jump, trying to catch my breath.

"Whoa, Thea, are you okay?" Finn says, voice hoarse. I'm still in his sitting room, breathing heavily, trying to catch my breath, he grips my shoulders, steadying me. Hali and Rowan are asleep beside us as the film credits roll over the screen.

"Did you watch it?" I asked.

"A bit. I fell asleep," he said running his fingers through his hair. "Did you just have a dream?" his arm still around me holding me tight.

"Yeah. I was in a cell." I said.

"A cell?" he said taking my hand to see for himself. "That's the Unseelie realm."

"She's going to arrest me?" I ask a little scared.

"I won't let anything happen to you." He said resting his head against mine.

"What if you can't stop it?" I ask honestly.

"Then I will do everything I can to get you back." He said, looking deep into my eyes. He leans down kissing me softly on the lips. "Come on. Let's get some sleep." He pulls me in tight, pulling the blanket up around my shoulders. His warmth encapsulating and calming.

Chapter 9

"WAKE UP!" Hali shouts, shaking me awake. I jump looking around but its only her and I in the room.

"What's wrong?" I panic, thinking something had happened.

"We need to get ready for the ball! We only have a few hours!" she shouts excitedly pulling me to my feet and to the room across the hall. The large bedroom was much like the rest of the castle, white marbled walls with large bed and a small red sofa stood at the foot of the bed. Three women waited for us, perched on the edge of a sofa, almost uncomfortable. They stand as we enter the room.

"This is Elenor, Harima and Greta. They will be helping us get ready." I nod at them each in turn and offer them an awkward wave. Elenor was a tall, slender woman with a crimson wave of hair flowing down past her hips in an intricate plait. Harima was a shorter woman with jet black hair and piecing violet eyes and Greta was the smallest. She was small framed, with bright white hair wrapped into a bun. The first thing I noticed were her shimmering wings, moving slowly and gracefully as if they had a life of their own, her pointed ears sticking out through her hair. All three wore royal blue toga style dresses. The royal colours.

"Please sit." Elenor gestures to the chairs in the middle of the room. Me and Hali sit side by side. The ladies immediately surrounded us and started touching our hair. Brushing it out and placing rollers in.

"Weird. I automatically thought that it would be magic." Hali chuckled.

"Somethings you just have to do the old-fashioned way." She smiled, grimacing when Harima brushed a little too hard.

"So, what will happen?" I asked.

"Well, people arrive early some people even arrive at noon. There is food, dancing and then when the sun starts to set all the guests head outside and starts the pollination. Then the party continues."

"What's the pollination?" She sighs as if it were obvious.

Which it is, sort of, except for the fact it's a single day event not a natural occurrence over a number of months.

"It would be easier for you to see it," she said, closing her eyes and relaxing. "So, Rowan told me what happened." She said giggling her eyebrows at me. "I knew you weren't going to step back. I knew you liked him," she said competitively, like she had won a marathon.

"It just got kind of out of control," I shrugged, my cheeks flaring. She jumped to look at me.

"Rowan said you were pinned up against the wall making out. Neptune only knows what would have happened if he hadn't interrupted," she said, the ladies behind giggled. My cheeks started to burn.
"It's just so hard! I don't know what to do. This is completely uncharted territory." I cover my cheeks trying to hide the embarrassment seeping from them.

"He really likes you," she said, settling back into her chair.

"I've never seen him act this way, and I have known him since I was a guppy."

"How do you know?"

"Well for one, he can't stop looking at you. Ever. Two, he arranged all of this." She gestures to the dresses hanging to the side, and the ladies behind us, "for you, and three, the way you two were last night. You fell asleep and he just pulled you in tighter. Like he didn't want to let you go." Her arms squeezing herself tightly, her voice sounding all dreamy. A little flutter started in my chest. The ladies behind all sighed in unison. This conversation was a little too public for my liking. "He didn't have a reason to stop the wedding before. But now he has." The ladies gasp as if they just realised who were talking about. Oh no.

"No, no, no. It's not like that. I didn't mean-." I panic trying to convince them I'm not trying to steal their Prince. Hali laughs. Elenor leaned towards me.

"No one wants this wedding. We don't like the Unseelie Royals. They are dark and evil. They will turn our beautiful lands sour, with their dark magic."

"The decision for this union was very out of the blue. No one saw it coming. We have been at odds with the Unseelie for millennia." Harima continued.

"We are glad the Prince has found someone he wants to be with, not being forced to be with," Greta added. I look around and they all nod in agreement. Even Hali. I let out a little sigh.

"That's all good but the King and Queen might not reconsider. Duty over Love." They all sighed almost in unison.

"Well, how about we make them change their minds?" Elenor said. "I am going to make you fit for a Prince. The belle of the ball." She clapped her hands and the girls worked faster, all giggling with excitement. She leaned in once more. "By the way your secret is safe with us." She said and placed her hand on my shoulder. As soon as she did, I could feel I could trust her.

"I would like to be a belle of the ball also." Hali says warily. The girls giggled and nodded.

After an uncertain amount of time, the woman helped us into our dresses and shoes. Then they came around to face us.

"A finishing touch." She said and she waved her hand face. The smell of vanilla filled the air. Harima waved her hand and a mirror appeared. Hali went towards it first.

"I feel so pretty." She said, almost tearing up. her hair was done into a bun with plaits and golden shells weaving around, her makeup was all golds and blues.

"You look so pretty!" I replied. She turned to me and gasped. Covering her cheeks.

"No, you do!" I headed towards the mirror. I looked twice; it didn't even look like me. my hair fell in loose curls, with the front pulled back out of my face in two plaits pinned over the top of my head. Like a hair tiara. A golden vein wrapped into them. My makeup was amazing. My checks glowed. When I turned the light shimmered off an almost invisible golden design on both temples. My crimson eyeshadow that faded into a white at the centre of my face with sleek black eyeliner. My lips crimson, with a slight sparkle in them.

"Never mind femme fatale. You look positively royal." She wiped a tear from her cheek.

"No, we look royal. Thanks to you three." I said, turning and taking Elenor's hands. "Thank you."

"No thanks necessary. It was our pleasure. You have a beautiful soul; we hope everything works in your favour." She winked and the three women left the room.

"How can she see my soul?" I asked Hali. She shook her head and giggled.

"Your Aura. Elenor can read peoples auras by touching them, different colours mean different things. That's a great compliment. Take it." she said. "Now we have a party to attend." She held her elbow out for me to link. I do and she takes me down the long corridor. As we near the main hall, Rowan is waiting at the door. He turns and catches sight of Hali. His eyes widen and so does his smile. He runs towards us and scoops her up, spinning her round.

"You look phenomenal," he says, as she lets out a little giggle. Her eyes are gleaming. I feel a little ache in my heart, they are just so happy. Rowan takes her arm and leads her away, but she turns to me.

"I don't want to leave Thea by herself," she says, pulling her arm gently away.

"No! You two go. I'm good." I smile shooing them away.
Rowan takes her arm back and offers me his free one.

"I'm enough man for two women." He puffs out his chest, proudly.

"You are too good to be true," she says, leaning behind him to make a scream face at me.

"You don't mind?" I ask, not wanting to intrude, but also not wanting to be left alone.

"Not at all. What wingman would I be if I let you wander around the single men?" he said with a wink. Hali pulls another face. one that said a quizzical *'interesting.'* I pull the same face back as he escorts us into the ballroom.

The smell of wildflowers hits me as we enter. The room is filled with bright and colourful flowers, trees and foliage. Bright colours, yellows, oranges and pinks have transformed the place into a meadow. Ferns, vines, blossom trees everywhere. I gasp. It 's incredible. Birds and insects are hovering overhead. I turn my attention to the guests. All unique, but all with pointed ears, wings fluttering with excitement. Hair of all colours. Everyone looked otherworldly. Which they were I suppose.

"It's amazing right?" Hali sighs.

"Is it always like this?" I ask.

"Yes, but it still feels amazing everytime." She smiled.

I catch sight of my grandmother, with a group of women. She excused herself and headed towards us.

"You girls are beautiful and have a lovely escort." She smiled at Rowan.

"You look amazing", Gran." She looked younger, happier. Almost ageless. Her silver gown glittered in the sunlight.

"Thank you. The Seelie air makes me feel good." She leaned in close. "Have you seen the Prince yet?" she asked. I could feel the grin on her face.

"Not today, why?"

"Well, I believe he's found you." She gestures behind me and returns to her friends. What do I do? Do I pretend like she didn't tell me and act natural? Do I turn? Do I go over to him? Before my tornado of questions have finished swirling in my head, Hali and Rowan turn to meet him, taking me with them.

He looked gorgeous. His royal blue suit made his eyes even greener. His hair tidied. I swear I melted into a puddle where I stood. His eyes widened, blinking and shaking his head.

"Finn!" Hali shouted. "Where have you been?"

"With the King and Queen." His smile widened and took my hands. "Planning a re-negotiation of the treaty with the Unseelie."

"You mean, you aren't getting married?" Hali said gleefully. My heart is pounding against my rib cage.

"Maybe one day." His eyes move to me. "But not to the Unseelie Princess." My heart burst. He pulled me in for a hug, squeezing me around the waist, his strong arms enveloping me, making me feel safe.

"That's great news!" Rowan said. Hali leaped on us, hugging us both.

"More than great!" she shrieked. "Now we can really celebrate. Let's dance." She lets us go and pulls Rowan to the dancefloor.

"Would you honour me with a dance?" he said bowing slightly.

"I'm not very good." I whispered pulling him back up and glancing around to see who was looking. By my count, everyone. He leaned in.

"I've seen your fighting. It's not much different, but I'll lead you," he said, holding out his arm to me. I take it and he leads me to the dancefloor. I catch sight of my grandmother, clasping her hands in front of her chest, with the *bless their hearts* look on her face. Everyone was looking.

"People are looking at you, what if I trip?" I panic. He chuckles.

"No, they're looking at you, and I won't let you fall." He smiles turning to face me and taking my hand.

"You're the Prince, they are looking at you. And probably wanting to kill me." I chuckle. "The outsider dancing with the Prince."

"No, they are looking at how gorgeous you are. The most beautiful woman in the room and their thinking 'how did he get so lucky?'" I all but swooned at that statement.

"Are you trying to say you like my dress?" I smiled.

"No, I'm saying you're beautiful. And I feel lucky to just be dancing with you." He smiled, gripping my hand tightly, as he starts to whisk me around the dancefloor, joining in near Hali and Rowan.

"Well I feel lucky, dancing with the handsome Prince." I said in my best fairy tale voice.

"So, you think I'm handsome?" he asks, raising a quizzical eyebrow, holding a smoulder.

"Of course. Otherwise I wouldn't be here," I winked.

"And here was me thinking you liked me for more than my looks," he smiled.

"Of course, but they are a definite bonus." I winked. He twirled me around and dipped me low, pulling me back up close to him before my head touched the floor.

"You're a good dancer." I smiled, slightly breathless.

"It's all about having the right partner."

"Will you two stop it? I can't concentrate with all the googly eyes." Hali joked, Rowan spinning her towards us.

"I can't help staring!" he scolded back at her.

"I know what you mean." Rowan seconded and they both laughed and high-fived. "Come on you pair, let's get a drink," he said leading Hali over to a fountain. Finn gripped me around my waist, and he spun us the whole way there.

"If dancing always feels like that, I should do it more often!" I say, gasping and slightly dizzy. He pulls away slightly hands on my hips to check I'm steady.

"You alright?" he laughs.
"Peachy." I smile as I looked as I pluck an apple from the bowl. Before I could bring the apple to my mouth Finn smacks it away, knocking it across the room.

"What did you do that for?" I asked, shocked.

"You can't eat the fruit. It will make you want to stay here forever. You won't be able to leave."

"Are we in Snow White?"

"They aren't poisonous, just too strong for humans." He smiled. "Anything else is fine." He handed me a glass shimmery pink liquid. I sipped delicately.

"I was wondering when you were going to get here." Hali said, waving as Eva and Rose walked towards us. "Do you want a drink?" she asked pouring another.

"No, thanks." Eva replied, shaking her head. She wore a deep olive-green dress with punky tulle skirt, with uneven layers. Rose wore a dark grey dress, with a high neck.

"You both look great." I said.

"Thanks," Rose replied, "though we didn't have a royal team to help us," she said sarcastically.

"You can tell," Hali replied, Taking my arm and pulling me away. "I don't know what's up with those girls. They were bitchy before but since you got here, they have gotten so much worse." Her brow wrinkled. "Come on, let's go powder our noses," she said, twitching it like a rabbit and giggling. We head back to the guest bathroom.

"I can't believe this place. It's so…"

"Magical." She wiggled her fingers in the air. "The magic between you two had everyone staring." She grinned.

"Stop! Were they really?" We turned into the bathroom.

"The magic was flying off you two! What did he say?" she smiled.

"He sa-." A shock hit me in the back of the head and darkness followed.

Chapter 10

I strain open my eyes, trying to strain to see through the blurred vision. My head pounding. A cold hard surface beneath me. I push myself up. Three stone walls and a wooden door. Oh Shit. My dream. I touch the back of my head where the pain radiates. Blood. I pull myself up and peer out of the tall barred window. Barren, dark. Is it night already? The rotten smells filling my nostrils. I run to the door. "Is anyone there?" Silence. Shit, shit, shit. What am I going to do?

"Uurgh!" Pulling on the door handle willing it open, falling back on my butt. I shiver, rubbing my arms for warmth. The cold floor barren of anything to ward off the cold. A door creaks down the hall.

"Hello?" I shout. Footsteps sounding towards me. Nearer and nearer. An ostrich egg sized eye fills the door bars. A cyclops?
"Oh, sleeping beauty has awoken." He sing songs in his dreary voice.

"Where am I?" I demand.

"These are your lovely chambers. We hope your stay in the Unseelie castle is an unpleasant one. However long it may be." He grinned showing his missing teeth, his bad breath filling my cell. His brown matted hair, stiff against his head.

"Why am I here?"

"Shut up! I'm not here to answer your stupid questions." He turned and walked further down the corridor.

"Was this the Princess' doing?" I shouted.

"Who else?" he shouted back. "Now stop pissing me off. She'll be here soon, and I don't want to damage you before she gets the chance." Shit. Of course, it was her. I need to get out of here. Think. I bang my head against the wall willing an idea to come to me. That's it! My head. I can't call Finn, he's at the ball and I don't want to get him into trouble. I'll call Hali on my telepathy phone. She already knows I'm missing, she was there when I was taken. Unless she isn't alright? Right, can't think like that. Head in the game.

Hali, are you there? Shit she can't answer. *I'm in the Unseelie prison. Send help. Hali please.*

I repeat it over and over again until my headache gets so bad, I can't concentrate. A door squeaks at the end.

"Hello? Hello!" I shout.

Footsteps head towards my door. Nearer and nearer. A key turns in the door. "I told you to shut up!" the cyclopes shouts raising his hand over his shoulder. I close my eyes, holding my hands up over my head, crouching down to protect myself. Fuck. A large thud next to me, then a clatter. Did he miss?

"Thea. Are you okay?" a pair of warm hands gently press against my shoulder and pull me up to standing.

"Finn?" I croak, open my eyes. He pulls his jacket off and wraps it around me, flooding me with warmth and relief. "Oh, thank god." He pulls me into a hug.

"Are you okay?" Finn asks.

"I'm fine, Is Hali okay?" I ask him. He keeps one hand firmly around my waist, supporting me, before stooping to collect his sword from the ground and guides me down the corridor, doors lining both sides. "Did you come alone?" I ask, my voice wavering.

"She's fine and no, Rowan is up ahead. He was watching the door."

As we reach the end, I see Rowan peering around a door, watching for guards.

"Let's get out of here." I say, trying to support myself.

"Theodora?" a weary voice sounds from inside the next cell. I pull myself up to look inside.

"Dad? Dad! I can't believe you're here!" Tears are filling my eyes as I try to reach my arm through. He is shackled to the wall by his hands and feet, skinny, drawn face, like he hasn't been fed properly in a while and he looked older. Much older than he should. Grey hairs streaking the sides of his head.

"I knew we would see each other again but you must go. Someone will be here soon." Panic flashed in his eyes. "I'm sorry, I didn't mean for you to get pulled into this, but your fate is more than I can control." His eyes dart to Finn.

"Finn, please, go find the keys." I ask, my voice shaking.

"No! You must go. She comes for you. You are the only one who can stop her." Footsteps sound in the distance. Finn turns my face towards him.

"We'll come back for him. We need to go now."

"I love you Thea." My dad's voice softens. My vision blurs, as the tears stream down my face.

"Finn, please I can't leave him." Almost a whisper, trying to hold in the sobs.

"Take her now!" my father shouts. Rowan grabs Finn's arm and with a buzz we are back at the castle, in Finn's sitting room.

"No!" I scream, falling to the floor.

"Go get Althea." Between the headache and travelling, I can't tell which ways is up. "It's okay. I got you." Finn swiftly picks me up, walks into his bedroom and places me on the bed. He immediately starts looking me over for injuries.

"We have to go back." I cry.

"We will. I'll get some guards together and we'll get him back Thea, I promise you." He leans and kisses me on the head. "Do you remember what happened?"

"No. I just woke up in that cell. How long was I gone?" I shiver. The adrenaline was wearing off.

"A few hours, I should have been there. I'm sorry." He sat down next to me and wrapped his arms around me trying to warm me up.

"How would we have known? Did Hali tell you where I was?" I asked.

"No, she was unconscious when we found her. Althea healed her but she was groggy. She gave her something to sleep." He pulled me closer, resting his head on top of mine. "After you didn't come back after a while, we got worried. My head was pounding and I knew something was wrong. We went to find you, and found Hali on the floor, but you were gone." He pulls back to look at me. "I thought you were dead."

"So, did I for a minute there." I let out a little laugh. Trying to stop the tears. "That cyclops really didn't like me. if you were a second later, I might have been a goner." his jaw clenched.

"How did you find me?"

"I don't really know. I looked everywhere. When I couldn't find you, I panicked. Then I heard your voice in my head asking for Hali to help you and my magic took me to you." He rubbed the back of his neck.

"Does it usually work like that?"

"No. Usually I would have had to have been to the place before. I just knew I had to get you back." He rested his hand against my cheek. My heart melting. "This was the dream you had last night, wasn't it?" I nodded gently. His fingers grazing the cut on the back of my head. I wince and he pulls away immediately.

"Shit." Looking down at his bloody fingertips. "You said you were fine." His brow furrows in worry.

"It's not that bad." My Grandmother hurries into the room.

"You had us all worried! We spent the whole party looking for you!" she said sitting down, on the other side of the bed.

"Her head." Finn says. I shoot him a look. He shoots me one right back. Hard to win.

"I'm fine."
"Uh huh." She is already separating the matted hair where my blood has dried in my hair. "You will be. Where's that healing potion I gave you?" she said sitting back and putting her hands on her hips.

"In the bag in the other room." Without instruction Finn goes to collect it.

"What happened?"

"The Unseelie Princess kidnapped me. I dreamt about it last night. She has Dad. He was shackled and skinny. I didn't want to leave him." My bottom lip started to tremble, threatening more tears.

"He's alive?" she let out a small sigh. "Things have escalated. We now know what you have seen will come to pass. She's probably using your father for his magic, or she's taken him so he wouldn't be able to warn the King and Queen." Finn returns with my bag.

"It's in the small zip pocket." I say, as he hands it to my Grandmother and she fishes for it. He returns to my side, wrapping a steady arm around my shoulders.

"Drink this and it will heal you right up. You will need to rest for it to work fully." I take the green vial and drink it quickly, holding the bridge of my nose. Surprisingly it tastes sweet. The pain in my head subsided immediately, leaving only drowsiness.

"She can stay here. She will be safe." He said, my grandmother gives him a *'she was literally just kidnapped from here'* look.

"I'm not going to let anything happen to her." There's a firmness in his voice.

"I understand. I'll be back in the morning. There is worse to come. I'll bring some things for you to help. You will need to practice more with your weapons. I'll get a spare healing tonic now and leave it in your bag."

"Okay. After what I just saw, I know I need the practice."

"Right, get some sleep." She stands to leave, bowing her head to Finn as she leaves.

"But, what about my Dad?" I ask, wearily.

"I'll get him back." He pulls me in and kisses me on the forehead. "Now get some rest, it's been a long day." He pulled the covers back and helps me under. He sat back down and pulled me in once more. "When you feel better, we will do some more training tomorrow afternoon." He cuddles in closer.

"You missed the ball!"

"So? I think there was more important things to be worrying about." He raised my chin with his finger to look into his deep green eyes.

"So, what happens at the pollination? Hali told me to wait and see but I missed it."

"How about I show you what happened last year?" he took my

hand and we closed our eyes.

A bell rings. "It is time for the annual Pollination," The King announces. He is a tall man, dark hair like Finn, a strong brow, and a large moustache. "A time where we celebrate life, love and hope for the future. The Queen and I would like to announce the joining of two realms through marriage. Our Son, Phineas has agreed to wed Brighid the Princess of the Unseelie, to end or feud and start anew!" The crowd gasps, whispering amongst themselves. "Please, join us outside as we start the Celebration." Everyone heads towards the door leading outside. The bright sun blinding as we cross the threshold.

"May the Pollination begin!" A trumpet sounds. Members of the crowd raise their arms in the air and a golden orb grows in the sky, growing and growing, expanding across the sky. When the golden orb has blocked out the sun and any remaining blue in the sky, the Queen draws he bow. The arrow sails through the sky bursting the orb on impact. Golden dust falls coating everything below. The flowers, the trees, the people. They all began to glow brighter and brighter. Finally bursting with life, the trees have fruit, the flowers are in full bloom and the people look healthier and younger.

"Wow." I open my eyes and meet Finn's gaze. I lean in and press my lips against his. He pulls away gently.
"Now, get some sleep." He says leaning back against the ornate headboard and pulling me into his shoulder. I nuzzle in and sleep takes me.

As I open my eyes, I reach and find an empty space next to me. I need to check on Hali. I climb out of bed, change out of this bulky ball gown and into my pjs and sneak across the hall. I crack open the door to the guest room. She's asleep. I back up slowly.

"Thea, is that you?" a groggy voice asks.

"Hali, I'm sorry, I didn't mean to wake you. I just wanted to make sure you're alright."

"Come give me a hug." She beckons. "I'm just so glad you're okay."

"I'm sorry you got hurt." I said.

"Please. It wasn't your fault!" I climb on the bed next to her. "Do you know where Rowan went?" she says looking around. "It's the middle of the night."

"No, Finn was gone too." Worry tugging at chest. "Should we go look for them?"

"No, we are safer here. Together." She pulls the duvet back for me to climb in.

"What happened?"

"Brighid happened."
"It was the Unseelie Princess? Because the wedding is off?" anger in her eyes.

"I presume so."

"Where did you go? Everyone was looking for you."

"She kidnapped me. Put me in the dungeon in the Unseelie realm. She has my dad."

"That bitch! He was in the dungeon with you?"

"Yeah, I saw him just before Finn pulled us out." My eyes start to burn with the impending water works.

"Oh honey. Come here." She pulls me in for a hug. "We will get him back." she pulled back. "Finn saved you? Again?"

"And Rowan."

"How did they know where to look?"

"Finn said he transported to me." Her jaw drops.

"You can't transport like that! Oh my Neptune. He found you based on thought of you alone. That's unheard of." Her eyes bulging from her head.

"Well, he can do it." I say shrugging.

"Do you know what this means?" physically vibrating.

"No, what?" the door bursts open, Rowan and Finn rush in wearing their armour and looking exhausted.

"Holy Fates! When you weren't in my room, I thought she came back for you." Finn said, both running to us.

"What happened?" I ask, confused.

"We went back to get your Dad." He sat next to me and I pulled him into a hug. He had blood smeared on his armour. I place my hands on his cheeks so I could look him over.

"He wasn't there, but a there were a few cyclops there waiting for us." Rowan answered.

"Thank you for trying. But you could have been killed. Both of you!" I looked over his body to check for injuries. His armour making my heart pounce. When I touch his ribs, he winced.

"That's what happens when you get punched by one." Rowan says. Hali hugging him around his waist and looking up at him longingly.

"Come on. It's my turn to look after you." Resting my forehead against his and getting lost in his eyes. "Are you okay?" I ask Rowan.

"No injuries to report. I had more sense, unlike pent up aggression over there. He barely let me get a hit in." He gestured to Finn. I stood up and wrapped his arm around my shoulders and took him back to his room.

"Goodnight guys, thanks again." I said closing the door behind us.

I sat him down on the sofa and started taking off his armour, it was easy enough with straps like a belt on the sides and under his arms, pulling it over his shoulders. He placed his hands on his ribs. His face pained. I place my hand on top of his.

"Let me help you." He nodded and released. I pulled off his t-shirt to check the damage. There weren't any cuts just a hell of a bruise. Probably broken ribs. I ran my fingers over his abs. My fingers tingling with every stroke.

My grandmother had left a vial of healing potion on the table. I uncorked the lid and handed it to him. "Drink this."

"No, I'm fine. That's for you."

"Drink up." I said tipping the vial into his mouth. "I'm fine." I stroked his face. "You had me worried." The bruise was fading already.

"I told you I would get him back."

"We will get him back. Together." I pulled his legs up on the sofa and I knelt beside him.

"I need to make sure you're safe." He said stroking my face. The feeling of comfort and longing was overwhelming. I closed my eyes.

"I need to make sure you're safe." I repeated back. He smiled.

"Come here." He pulled me into his lap, hugging me to his chest. "I don't know what it is about you, Thea. The dreams let me see a glimpse, but now having you here, I just can't let anything happen to you. When you were gone…" I rest my chin on his muscular chest and look up into his eyes.

"I'm okay. I'm safe. You're safe. Now come on. We need to get some sleep." He wraps his arm around me, sweeping me up into his arms in one swift motion. I let out a little gasp.

"Hey! Your meant to be resting." flicking some dirt out of his hair. He walks us into his bedroom door.

"You can sleep in here." He says, placing me back in bed. "I'll take the sofa." kissing me on the forehead. His warmth and tenderness making me feel weak as a lamb. I grab his hand. A volt of fear shooting through me. Fear for being alone and being back in the dark damp dungeon.

"Stay with me?" he smiles, and I scoot over, he climbs in wrapping his warm arms around me. Protecting me in his embrace. A tingling sensation covers my body and I drift off.

Chapter 11

Getting up has never been more difficult than when your cuddling and don't want the moment to end, but the weight of his arm had mine going to sleep. The morning sunlight was seeping through the window, and that was all the encouragement I needed to get to work. I have never felt vulnerable before, I never needed to, but now I needed to be prepared. I slide from under Finn's arm, trying not to wake him, freezing when he wriggles a little. I write a little note and place it on the bed next to him, not wanting to worry him. I pull on my gym clothes from Friday and head straight to the armoury. I need to practice. I pick up the daggers, a bow and a sword and head out to the target. Throwing the daggers consistently at the target, improving my aim with every shot, increasing the distance every so often for more of challenge. Again and again, until I moved on to the bow. Drawing the bow, like Hali taught me. pushing all I had into it.

"Getting there." A familiar voice sounded from behind. I turn to see Gran lingering by the door.

"How did you find me?"

"The guard saw you head out here. He's been keeping an eye on you to make sure you don't take your eye out."

"So not doing too well at sneaking then." I laughed, placing the bow on my shoulder.

"Come here. I brought you something." She gestures to follow her into the armoury.
"These are for you." She opens the bag up and reveals her armour, sword, daggers and shield. "They looked after me when I needed

them. Now it's time for me to hand them down to you. This battle is coming. From what happened yesterday, I don't think we can avoid it anymore," she said, placing her hand on my shoulder. "One more thing. I have bought you a spell that allows you to store objects in the ether."

"The what?"

"The ether is sort of a place between realms. This spell will allow you to store your weapons and a satchel there so you can access it anywhere at any time. Saves you carrying it everywhere!" she giggled, placing her hand on her back.

"How do I access it?"

"Firstly, let me do the spell." She took out a piece of paper and started reading the incantation. She took my hand and pierced my first finger. As the blood oozed out, she wiped it on each weapon in turn then the satchel they were placed in. once she finished, they all disappeared. "There. Now think of the object you want and call to you."

I closed my eyes and concentrated on the daggers, with a flash, they were in my hand. "Cool! How do I send them back?"

"Same concept but reversed! Imagine them disappearing into the ether." I shut my eyes again and the weight of the daggers faded from my hands.

"That is probably the coolest present I have ever been given," I said, hugging my grandmother. "Thank you."

"That's not all. Please get the satchel." I called on the satchel and when it appeared, I handed it over. "I have filled this with potions. I have labelled each one, so you know what they are. It will take a lot more lessons before you know what each of them look like. For now, though I would like you to read this book. It has some of the most important potions you will need in them. Study up and I will test you tomorrow." She placed a large lavender bound book into my palms. It had an intricate black insignia on the front. My arms drop with the weight.

"A quiz on all this, tomorrow?"

"Just read what you can. We'll see how far you get and have a go at making a few." She hugs me and turns to leave. "Will you be back tonight?"

"I think so." I shrug. I need more clothes anyway, I've run out, and I need to take them home and give them a wash.

"Okay. Casserole for dinner." She heads for the door and turns abruptly. "One more thing. Those weapons will always return to the ether. So, if you throw a dagger and don't retrieve it, it will return to the ether. See you at home, sweetie."

Chapter 12

Brighid

I pace in front of the fireplace. That bitch. She thinks she's won. That half breed really thinks she has beaten me? Well she has made a big mistake coming here and disrupting my plans. A revenge she will never see coming because if I have anything to do with it, she won't be living.

The guard hustles into the room with a bound man.
"So glad you could join us. Now, tell me, what do you see?" I curl my fingers into a wide fist, unleashing the painful mind control magic I have. What's great about it is how painful it is to his kind. Dream weavers. He writhed on the floor in pain. I smile at the carnage.

"There is nothing you can do now. They are- fated. You can't come between them!" he screams, I press my lips together in displeasure.

"Fated? They're fated!" I throw a fire ball against the wall leaving a dark scorch mark, it soothes me, somewhat. "How?"

"She is able to share dreams with him, before they met. She is able to send him messages with ease, he feels her pain and she makes him stronger. You can no longer stand between them. She may be only half Fae but she is stronger than I. Stronger than many with him beside her. If you cross them, you will die."

An idea flickers like a spark in my brain.

"If they are stronger together, than I will separate them. They don't know this yet and she is so trusting, she will believe it when she hears he has chosen me. Especially if it comes from that little sea nymph." I smile victoriously. "As you say, they feel eachothers pain and we all know, one mate cannot live without the other."

"No, please! Leave her alone!" He battles against the guards restraining him. I flick my wrist at the guards and they drag him from the room. For a man I have barely been feeding for the past two years, he surprises me.

"Now it's time for a new plan and a new potion. I'm going to break her heart before I rip it from her chest."

Chapter 13

As I lay on my bed, I have nearly finished half the book my grandmother gave me. Surprisingly, I have enjoyed reading it more than I thought. The number of spells that would have helped me over the years, I wish I knew this stuff earlier.

"Are you ready dear? We have about an hour until your mother gets home," my grandmother shouts up from the bottom of the stairs.

"I'll be down in a second!" I close the book, tucking it neatly under my arm as the mirror pulses three times.

I hesitantly move towards it and tap on the glass and Finn's face comes through, pacing my dad's old chambers. I step through the portal.

"Are you alright?" I ask, placing my hand on his shoulder to turn him towards me. He stiffens, before turning towards me.

"I thought you weren't home." He rubs the back of his neck, uncomfortably.

"So why were you knocking?" I raise an eyebrow.

"Okay, I just wanted to see If you would go out with me tomorrow? I want to show you something." Taking a step towards me and placing his warm hand against my cheek. The contact making my skin tingle and warm.

"That sounds perfect." I smile. "But I have to head off now, Gran is making me study the potions and testing me on what I have learned." He kisses me softly on the forehead before kissing my cheek and finally my lips.

"See, now tomorrow seems too long to wait." Murmuring against my lips. I giggle before lightly smacking his chest, before pulling him in for one more kiss. He pulls me firmly against the hard plains of his chest before pushing me away with his eyes closed.

"If I look at the kissable face of yours one more time, I'm never going to let you leave. You should go before I change my mind," he says seriously, with a joking undertone.
I place a soft kiss on his cheek before scurrying back through the mirror.

"There you are! Couldn't stay away could you?" My gran wiggles her eyebrows giving me a knowing look. I feel the crimson flush my cheeks.

"Don't we have a test or something?" I change the subject, moving past her to head down the stairs.

"Yes, without a moment to lose! How far did you get?"

"I got to the section on using mistletoe berries in an antidote to most poisons, which intrigues me as mistletoe is poisonous." She nods in understanding.

"Some things, when made into the right concoction can be something entirely different." I raise my brow at her.

"Did that even make sense?"

"Maybe not in this world," she winks
.
As we get to the kitchen, I can see she has laid out ingredients ready on the kitchen table, the stove is pre-heated and the kettle is boiling.

"Right. We are going to work on defensive potions as they are the most important. We will make a few more healing potions, location tonics, protection charms, and also a sleeping tonic. So, let's get started. We'll start with a protection charm. These usually last 12 hours and you can't take more than three in a row. You are going to need to grab the Lavender, Aloe vera and Jasmine to start." she says pointing towards the arranged table. I flick through the vials and collect the ones needed before adding them into the mortar. Once grounded I boil them in sea water, adding a little magic and watch the white cloud of smoke spill over the sides of the pan like smoke from dry ice. "Great job."

I turned out making the potions came easier to me than cooking. I was always an awful cook, always burning, overboiling or adding to much of an ingredient to make it taste disgusting but this, this feels like I was meant to do it.

"Hey, maybe next you could teach me how to make a good carbonara." I laugh. Gran raises her eyebrow and nods awkwardly.

"I'd like to try one more thing," she says, placing the last of the vials in the cabinet. "I want to work on your telepathy. I know we have already practiced, but this time, I want you to read my mind," she says, taking a seat at the table.

"That isn't something I have been able to do before."

"I know, I know. Just humour your Gran. Come, sit," she says pulling out the chair next to her. I follow suit and she takes my hand, closing her eyes. "Now clear your mind. This is different to sending messages, but not too different to seeing what another person is doing. So, clear your mind and think of me. Think of how we are connected. Now find the right station and tune in."

I close my eyes and picture my gran. I imagine the little tv box that is her mind, but instead of tv screen like before, I imagine an old radio. I flick through the channels slowly until I pick up a line. *'Chicken, mushroom'* .. what?

"Chicken and mushroom?" I laugh, and Gran joins me.

"Close. I was asking whether you preferred a chicken or mushroom carbonara. The more you practice the clearer it will get."

"To be honest, I don't really want to read people's minds. It just doesn't feel right."

"It doesn't have to be so invasive. By opening up this door, it will allow you to read people's intentions, their feelings and when they are lying. It's a good trick to have."

"I suppose that's not too invasive."
"Just make sure you practice. Physical contact helps. I think you should make sure to keep that door open for the foreseeable future. It may save your life."

"Good point. It may mean I have to make awkward contact with people, but I need to know who the unseelie Princess's spies are." My Gran nods in response, rising from the table to put the kettle on.

"Oh look, Len has a friend." Gran smiles, pointing to the window. I go to look, only to find a yellow canary.

Chapter 14

I take one last look in the mirror before I leave for my date with Finn. I smooth out the wrinkles in my white floral summer dress and check my make-up.

"You need to tell him. He needs to be prepared." My grandmother says, from her perch on the end of my unmade bed, Toby curled up on her lap.

"I know, I just don't want to ruin this day. I'll tell him straight after our date, I promise," I assure her. I feel guilty for not telling him about the yellow canary, but there is a chance that dad's prophecy was wrong. What if I told him and ruined our date for it all not to be true? I just want one normal day with Finn, no kidnappings, no near drownings, just me and him.

"Please be careful."

"I will, I promise." And with that the mirror pulses. "I'll see you later." I give her a quick hug and Toby a scratch on the head, before slipping through the mirror.

"Wow you look great!" Finn says, pulling me in and kissing me on the cheek. He is wearing a crisp, white shirt with blue jeans his ebony hair, carefully combed back, his green eyes piercing. He holds out his hand to me revealing a bright orange flower I have never seen before.

"Thank you, you clean up well yourself." I wink at him, leaning in to smell the flower and inhaling the intoxicating scent. As I go to take it, he pulls it back quickly, before gently placing it behind my ear, his hands lingering, before sweeping down my neck.

"Mmmm, why does it smell so good?"

"Everything here is meant to entice you in," he says seductively against my ear.

"So, is that what is going on here? It's not you I'm attracted to, it's this place." I quirk my eyebrow.

"Possibly." He laughs to himself. He runs his fingers against my bare arms, goose bumps rising in his wake. "But I think I'm the only one to have this kind of effect on you, regardless of where we are." He places delicate kisses on my neck as I try to stifle a moan. He pulls away reluctantly. "We should really get going otherwise we may never leave."

"We could stay a little longer." I jump up sitting on the desk, he comes to stand in between my knees.

"You, my siren, are going to be the death of me." He says, before firmly planting his lips against mine, pulling me tight to his chest, I can feel the hard plains of his abs through his shirt. I sigh internally. He swipes his tongue across my lower lip before dipping it into my mouth. His hands exploring my body. A warmth starting to pool in my core. "We should really go; I have the whole day planned out." He groans, both of us trying to catch our breath.

"Okay," I say reluctantly before following him down the stairs and out to the courtyard of the castle. He leads me a little further out of the castle walls to the river where a water carriage waits, drawn by horses that were completely clear. Upon closer inspection I realised they were made of the water itself.

"They are called Ceffyl Dwr, or water horse in English. Don't get too close, they are menacing creatures." I take a step forward placing my hand near one of the horses and get a sense of him.

"I can feel his mischief." I smile, Finn raises a quizzical eyebrow.

"Really? These guys are known for being pests. Even murderous in some regions." My mouth gapes in shock as he leads me to the water carriage. The plush cushions look out of place in the aqueous environment. "Don't worry they are fine on the Fae plane. When did you learn to do that?"

"Yesterday with Gran. She had me practice all night reading her mind." He motions and the carriage begins to glide through the water.

"Can you read mine?" He smirks, leaning in and wiggling his eyebrows.

"I don't really like to read people minds. It feels invasive and makes me feel gross. It's easier for me to read peoples intentions instead."

"So, what are my intentions then?" he whispers against the collar of my neck.

"Indecent ones. Definitely not first date appropriate." We both laugh.

"Go on. Read my mind. Tell me what I'm thinking." His forehead wrinkles in concentration.

I place my hand on his, he flips his and laces our fingers together, sending a warm sensation shooting up my limbs. I close my eyes and tune in. *Beautiful.*

"All I heard was beautiful. I can't really pick up full sentences yet."

"Well I guess I could fill in the blanks. I was saying how beautiful you looked. Even more beautiful than the first time I met you."

"That was only a week ago," I laugh, "and you're only saying that because I look more Fae now."

"No, I don't think that's it. I think you would have caught my eye whatever you were. Even if you were an ogre. It's your light. You seem brighter now." He kisses me gently on the cheek.

"I feel like I know myself more, the dreams always were a mystery to me, but now I know where they come from, it kind of explains all the little holes in my life."

The carriage slows to a stop as we come to a lagoon, resting against the side of a vast cliff, the top indistinguishable from the clouds, a vibrant blue waterfall spilling over the side. Large colourful flowers cling to the sides of the cliff face. Blues, pinks, purple and oranges. The same flower he gave me at the castle.

"It's gorgeous! I exclaim covering my mouth as I gasp.

"I thought you'd like it. You may not be a water nymph, but I saw the way you were in the ocean." He takes my hand and leads me over to the edge of the turquoise water. I slip off my shoes, dipping a toe, I pull back quickly expecting it to be cold but surprisingly find it is quite refreshing.
He pulls a bag from behind his back and hands it to me. "I thought we could go swimming. It's safe here." I open it to a yellow bikini and a towel.

"Where did you get this?" I smile. He rubs the back of his neck. The movement I know he does when he feels nervous or embarrassed.

"I had a little help. I wanted it to be a surprise, so I asked Hali to get it for you. I hope you don't mind. There is a little cabin just down that path, you can go there to change if you'd like."

"This is great, thank you! I'll be right back." I kiss him firmly against his cheek before scurrying in the direction of the path. I stop short of the cabin and gaze in wonderment. Small he said. This could fit at least four families comfortably. I chuckle internally before heading inside and making quick work of changing into my bathing suit. I must admit, Hali did a great job. The colour makes my skin glow and fits like a glove! I'm just happy she picked something plain, since Hali picked it, I'm a little shocked it's not sparkly. I head out, towel draped over my arm to where Finn is treading water, looking at the flower adorned cliff face. I stroll in, the cooling water getting deeper faster than I thought it would, within a few steps I am up to my thighs. He turns when he hears the water displace in my wake.

"Is it wrong if I say I prefer you better in this than the dress?" he smirks. I stop, placing a hand on my hip.

"It wouldn't be wrong, no. It may be not be very Princely of you," I say, curtsying into the water, before swimming up to him.

"Princely, huh?" he says, meeting me halfway, wrapping his muscular arms around my waist.

"Like gentlemanly, but on a whole other level." I have a mocking tone to my voice. I try to keep a straight face, but the wide smile that splits his cheeks, makes my insides turn to goo and is completely infectious. We both stand there, grinning at each other, before he leans in kissing me firmly, before pulling away and resting his head in the crook of my neck.

"I don't know how I have lived without you for so long. Where have you been all my life?" he murmurs against my skin, tingling the nerve endings, sending waves of euphoria, through me. That familiar heat racing to my core. Also trying not to get the Rihanna song stuck in my head.

"Would it be too cheesy if I said I was in your dreams?" I laugh to myself.
"Maybe, but it does make you the literal girl of my dreams," he says, lifting his head up, cupping the back of my neck in his hands, caressing the nape.

"Does that make us weird? We knew each other before we met, we have this amazing connection and I feel more comfortable with you than anyone I have ever me," I ask, searching his eyes for an answer. He kisses me softly again.

"No, it makes us incredibly lucky that we found each other."

He pulls me tighter against him and I instinctively wrap my legs around his waist. His eyes have darkened with lust as he kisses me again, harder than before, slipping his tongue between my lips as his hands find the curve of my butt. I get lost in the feeling of him, I run my fingers over his muscular shoulders and up into his damp hair, pulling my nails along his scalp, which elicits a soft moan from him. His hands move desperately up my torso and cup my breasts in his hands. He slips his fingers beneath the material, moving his mouth to the column of my neck leaving a scorched trail in his wake. The water starts to dance around us, spinning and swirling, brushing against my heated skin. His words slipping through my brain without any effort from me. *Perfect, gorgeous, soft, amazing, love.* Not really coherent sentences, but they come to me with ease, as the tether that connects us grows thicker and stronger with every encounter.

"Your Highness," comes a voice from the edge of the lagoon. Finn curses under his breath, burying his face into my neck.

"What?" he shouts menacingly. I look over to the guard who has taken a few steps back.
"The King and Queen have requested your presence immediately," he says, much quieter than before.

"You have got to be kidding me," he mutters under his breath, before shouting back, "Can this wait? I told them today was important and to only be contacted in case of an emergency."

"No, your Highness. It cannot. They said it is a great matter of urgency and sent for you immediately. They would like to speak to you." He says dipping his head in apology. "Alone." He adds. Finn growls into my neck.

"Okay, tell them I am on my way. I just need to return Thea to her house." I realise my legs are still entwined around his waist, so I hastily untangle myself. He takes my hand and leads me to shore.

"I'm sorry, Your Highness. The King requested you return alone, and I return Miss Theadora to the human realm."

"Absolutely not. I will take her back. I need to make sure she is safe," he says pulling me closer. I grip his chin and turn it to me.

"I'll be fine. It must be an emergency if they sent for you, so you need to get back, please. I'll be fine." I kiss him lightly on the cheek, before turning and exiting the lagoon and collecting my things. He rushes forward and grips my wrist.

"Please, Theadora. Just let me make sure your safe." His eyes are pleading.
"I'll be fine. It's an emergency, Finn, you need to go." I take a step away and towards the guard. "Hold out your hand." He hesitantly raises it and I take it firmly, which makes the guard stiffen before accepting. I close my eyes for a minute before dropping his callous hand and turning back to Finn. "He is loyal to you and your family. You can trust him. If there is anything wrong, I will call out," I say, tapping the side of my head.

Finn sighs before stepping up to me and placing his forehead on mine. "Still, let me know when you are home safe. I need to know, otherwise I can't think straight. I'm sorry our date got cut short."

"I will. Anyway, we have plenty of time for a rain check. Now, go. They need you," I say, kissing him on the cheek and taking a reluctant step back. He flashes a stern look to the guard before he blinks out of existence.

"So how do I get home from here. Are we going to take the carriage back to the castle?" I ask, pulling my dress over my head.

"We will not be returning to the castle, miss." He says, his head turned the other direction.

"Then how will I get home? I need to use the mirror."

"There are gateways in nature. There is one near the cabin down the path. That is why the cabin was placed there. A crevice in the cliff wall takes you back to the human plane," he informs me.

"Can it take me anywhere?" I ask.

"No. They are more like doorways. Only one destination." He starts down the path and I follow him.

"Has something bad happened at the castle?" I ask, concern lacing my voice.

"I'm not sure miss. I was just sent for the Prince. I wasn't informed of why." I nod in understanding, gnawing at the side of my cheek. "I'm sure it is nothing to worry about Miss." He assures me.

"Thank you, I'm sorry, what Is your name?" I ask, a little shyly.

"Bran, miss." He says a little shocked. "You're the only one who has asked my name." I look at him, shocked, he gestures to the wide crack in the cliff face. "This should take you out in a place called Bosherston. Is that okay, Miss?" he asks sincerely.

"That's fine, depending on where in Bosherston. "I say laughing. Tthank you for your help Bran. It was nice to meet you." He smiles sincerely and cobalt eyes shine.

"It was a pleasure to meet you too, Miss Theadora. I hope to see you again soon," ,e says as I step through the portal. With a zap, whizz and a pop I find myself on Broad Haven beach, exiting through the cliff face. I walk back up to the pathway that leads out into Bosherston village, along the path until I get to the tea rooms and then turn towards Stackpole. The benefits of visiting my grandmother in the summers was the walks we went on, most of them not a stone's throw away from our doorstep and within walking distance. The lily ponds being one of my gran's favourites means I know the way home like the back of my hand. Now I'm thinking it wasn't just the scenery she was coming here for. She was coming her for the doorway.

∞∞∞

Within 20 minutes, I am walking through my front door, much dryer than I was when I first put my dress back on, but my hair in a clumpy mess. Gran looks up from her chair.

"How did you get home?" she asks me confused. She looks down at her watch. "You've only been gone three hours; I wasn't expecting you back this early. Is everything alright?" she asks getting up to check on me.

"I'm fine. Finn had to go back to the castle for an emergency. I used the doorway at Bosherston to get back and just walked home." She gives me a stern look.

"You shouldn't be out walking by yourself; you should have called. You know the dangers that are lurking at the minute!" she brings her glasses down her nose to scold me good and proper.

"I was fine, Gran." I assure her. "There have been no problems all day."

The letter box sounds, and Toby rises from his slumber on the sun-baked tiles in the kitchen to race to the front door, barking at the intrusion.

"The postman has already been today." Gran says, racing past me to beat Toby to the delivery. She returns with a solemn look on her face.

"What is it Gran?" I say peering at the blue and gold envelope in her hand.

"An invitation." She and the card to me. "To the Royal wedding."

Chapter 15

"Maybe they sent it before the wedding was cancelled." I say pacing the living room. I have tried to call out to Finn, but there feels like something is blocking it. I can't see where he is either. It's taking everything in me not to panic, yet, I am still panicking.

"Invitations are sent through a portal dear. They are almost instant. I'm so sorry," she says, stepping into my path and wrapping her arms around me.

"There has to be something wrong. He wouldn't do this willingly," I say shaking my head. There's a knock at the door and I pull away to answer it. I am greeted with a sombre looking Hali stood at the door.

"I'm so sorry Thea," she says, paying more attention to her shoes.

"You of all people should know that something is wrong. I was with him not thirty minutes ago and he was fine!" I shout.

"I just spoke to him Thea. I'm sorry. I don't know what else to say. He said his duty has to come first. He said, he simply changed his mind." I stare at her struck dumb. A tear makes a path down her cheek.

"Changed his mind?" my voice barely a whisper. "I need to speak to him." I take the stairs two at a time and get to my bedroom in record time.
"Thea. Please, wait." I go to step through the mirror but hit a wall. "He blocked access through the mirror." Hali whimpers, tears streaming down her cheeks at this point. I sit on the floor and stare at the mirror. She sits down next to me and places an arm

around my shoulders. "I'm so sorry Thea. I don't know why he is doing this. I thought... I thought..." she cried.

"What Hali?!" I shout, making her jump back. My grandmother finally makes it to the bedroom, Toby at her feet. I touch the mirror again, my hand still not going through. I drop my hand back into my lap.

"I thought you were fated," she murmurs.

"What did you just say?" I ask, turning to her.

"Fated. It's an old legend we have in our land. Some Fae have these connections, sort of like true love, I suppose. It makes them stronger. They can communicate mentally and share emotions and feelings with each other. They know when the other is in danger. All the signs were there."

"But there hasn't been a fated match in centuries, Hali." Gran interrupts. "But I thought the same thing. The dreams, the shared mental link, the feelings. You're right, the signs were all there dear, but it can't be the case. A fated couple cannot live without each other once the connection has begun. The body will reject any other advances, even make you physically sick the longer you are apart." I dip my head into my hands and cry.

"Did I do something wrong?"
"No, Oh Neptune no. He's a jerk and I wish I never encouraged you," she cried, pulling me into a hug.

"I'm going to make you girls some tea," Gran says, placing her hand briefly on my shoulder before heading back down the stairs.

Hali and I sit in front of that mirror hugging for what seems like forever. I feel stupid, angry, naive to have even thought that Finn could like me. I let my dreams cloud my judgement and he just said all the right things. What is that saying? 'So many girls fall in love with the wrong guy simply because he says all the right things.' I wish that were the case, but I can't imagine myself with anyone else. My heart feels like it's been ripped in two and they will never fit perfectly back together.

"Come on. I have an idea. We are going to spend the night watching films and talking crap about him and eating a mountain of junk food, that I will acquire. What do you think?" Hali says, standing up and shuffling through her pockets for her keys.

"Sounds good." I smile, weakly. She gives me a pitying look.

"Great, what's your favourite snack. Scratch that, I'm just going to get one of everything. I'll be back in a blink." She says heading down the stairs.

I place my hand against the mirror, willing it to work.
"Please Finn. Please," I murmur to the reflective glass, realising how desperate and broken I looked. I didn't feel this way at all when I broke up with Nick and we had been together for a year. In a moment of adrenaline, I rise and push the mirror against the wall, cracking it, before collapsing back on to the floor.

"Thea! What are you doing?!" My grandmother shouts, her feet making quick work of the stairs. "Oh Thea, honey," she says, picking up the mirror and hugging me.

"No, I'm fine." I say shaking my grandmother off me. "I just need a minute. I need a good scream."

"Then scream," she says. I stare at her for a minute and then scream. Scream for myself, scream for Finn, scream for my Dad. Hali runs up the stairs.

"Holy Neptune! I thought you had died. I swear I heard you down the street!" she says shaking her head. "Feel better?" she gives a small smile. I nod a little. "Good because I brought the snacks, so slap a movie on the TV and let's start there and see how far we get." She says emptying the contents of the bag onto the bed. She really did get one of everything. Every chocolate bar, packet of crisps and any type of snack she could find.

I grab a bag of chocolate M&M's and crawl under my duvet. She picks out 'Bridesmaids' and plonks it in the DVD player, as she says in the voice of Kristen Wiig "let's get ready to paaarrttaayy."

I open the bag and inhale the chocolatey scent. Hali, pulls back the duvet and crawls in next to me.

"I'm here if you need me," she says, patting the duvet over my hip. I watch up until the scene where Annie breaks the giant cookie at the bridal shower. I have thoroughly eaten myself into a chocolate coma, and I close my eyes.

Opening my eyes again, I find I'm back by the lagoon. Finn is swimming around in circles, while I watch him from the shore dipping my toes in the crystal blue waters.

"Glad you could finally join us," Brighid's voice beckons from the shade of a tree. The ground turns dark and dead and the water turns a putrid shade of green.

"What's going on?" I look out to Finn and he's making his way towards her, the putrid green water giving off the smell of rotten eggs and sewerage as it parts for him. "Finn?"

"He can't hear you. I just wanted to have this little chat with you. Your Father is quite the conduit." I can't look at her. I watch as Finn, strides out of the water and stands in front of her, stroking her cheek, affectionately.

"Please Finn," I beg. He doesn't move.

"You see, I need Finn for my plan to work. He is mine. Well, until I have no use for him anymore. But hey, I might as well enjoy this fine specimen of a man whilst I have him." She snickers and steps out from underneath the tree so she is toe to toe with Finn. "Don't even think abut stopping the wedding tomorrow, he is lost to you now. The consequences if you meddle in my plans will be... fatal." She grabs his face with her grey, bony hands and drags his face towards hers. Before their lips touch, I find myself back in my bed, leaning over the side dry heaving.

"Holy Fates! What's wrong?" A voice cries. "Althea!" I feel Hali, hold back my hair, as the creak of the stairs gives me a warning of my grandmother's presence.

"Another dream?" she asks, once I have managed to stop. I nod weakly.

They both take my hands and I show her what happened. She frowns. "That was no dream. That was a message."

"Something is wrong with Finn. I could feel it. He was the same way in the vision of the wedding. She's already got her spell on him, I know it."

Hali nods in understanding. "We don't have much time. I will go to the castle and check on him. The guards have orders to not let you into the castle," she says, heading for the stairs.

"We still have a few days, until the wedding. We have to stop this!" I shout.

They both share a concerned look.

"What aren't you telling me?" My gran takes my hand and kneels in front of me.

"Thea, you have been asleep for two days. It's Friday night. The wedding is tomorrow."

Chapter 16

"Happy Birthday, Thea!" my mother says rushing into the room. I smile at her as she sits on the edge of my bed and hands me a large, rectangular present, beautifully wrapped in red paper with a big white bow on the top.

"Thanks, Mum." I smile and begin to unwrap the present as Gran, makes her way upstairs. Slower than usual, for my mother's benefit. I rub the layers of sleep from my eyes. For a girl who slept for two days, I feel exhausted.

Hali had left to check on Finn. I haven't heard back from her since, which scares me more than I care to think about. My gran gives me a brave face, joining my mother on the end of my bed.

"I'm sorry I haven't been here lately. The job has really pulled me under, and when I get home you're either at Hali's or already asleep." She gives me a weak smile.

"Sorry Mum." She swats away my apology.

"Don't apologise. I'm so glad you have found some friends and it's not like I'm here most of the time anyway." She smiles again, pushing stray hairs from her powdered cheeks.
I finish unwrapping the present to reveal a gorgeous silver dress. A modest V-neck with flowy shoulder capped sleeves. As I lift it out of the box, I can see that it's a wrap dress, the skirt is loose fitted and comes to around mid-calf.

"Gran mentioned attending a wedding today. I thought you might need a new dress for the occasion." Her sweet gesture constricts my heart, and it takes everything in me not to cry.

"Thank you, Mum, I love it." I smile and hug her tight.

"Mine next," my grandmother says, handing me a box of a similar size to the one my mother gave me. As I open it up, I see a long white cloak, that sparkles in the sunlight. "It was mine. I thought you could bring it with you in case you get cold." She winks at me.

"Cold? It's July!" my mother laughs.

"Still, it is an outdoor wedding," Gran says moving back to the staircase. "I'm going to start your special pancake breakfast." She nods.

"Thank you, this will go lovely with my dress." I smile.

"You had best start getting ready, I will bring your pancakes up to you in around 20 minutes." She smiles before heading downstairs. As she opened the door at the bottom, I hear the clatter of claws as Toby bounds up the stairs and straight onto the bed, waggling his butt for affection. I quickly oblige.

"Are you looking forward to the wedding?" my mother asks. I can't blame her. She knows nothing.

"Yes, it should be lovely." I feel myself smile but it doesn't reach my eyes.

"How did you get an invite?"
"It's a family friend of Hali's. I'm her plus one." Mum nods once in understanding.

"Well I hope you have a great day. I'm going to be heading into the office this morning, so hopefully I will see you when I get home?"

"I'm not sure. I might be staying at Hali's; in case we get back too late."

"Of course. I will see you tomorrow then." She makes her way across the room, before turning again. "How about next Saturday we spend the day together? We can do whatever you want?"

"That would be great, Mum." I smile, and she returns with her very own, before she leaves the room.

The day I have dreaded most has finally arrived. I get up starting to get ready for the mayhem that is about to unravel. The fact that Hali didn't comes back, leads me to believe she is under the control of Brighid now, just like my dream showed me she would be. If anything happens today, I want to make sure everyone I love is safe, away from the tyranny of Brighid's reign. I pray everyone will come out of this unscathed, that Finn won't marry her and maybe we can save my father. I know, I am trying to be optimistic. After a quick shower I start on my face. I'm going for a blending in effect at this wedding so I go for a natural look. I dry my hair and start to heat up the curling tongs. As I wait, I glance at the clock. 11:15. I have an hour before I need to be out of here.

"You look beautiful, dear," Gran says, walking into my room with a pile of chocolate chip pancakes with maple drizzle and a candle in the top. She sets the steaming pile of deliciousness in front of me and I blow out the candle. "Now eat them up. You'll need your energy." She smiles, half-heartedly.

"Thank you." I take a forkful and let the sweet sugary taste coat my tongue, savouring it. I let out a soft moan of gratitude.

"I really don't like this plan of yours, but you are a woman after my own heart. I know if I don't help you, you will do it alone anyway," she sighs. "That cloak I gave you earlier. It is enchanted. When you wear it, you will not be able to be identified. Just another face in the crowd. Wear it for as long as you can," she says, sitting on the edge of my bed. "Have you heard from Hali yet?"

"No, I think she's under the spell."

"I thought so. Just please promise me. If things get bad you will not do anything rash. You need to be safe," she implores.

"I will." I lie.

"Time to go sweetheart." I make my way down the stairs to where Gran stands ready in the kitchen. "You look wonderful dear." She smiles. She is wearing a burgundy dress, with a long full skirt, her hair, intricately wrapped into small circles at the base of her skull. "These transportation charms will take us to just outside the castle walls, from there, we will join the crowd of people making their way to the castle for the ceremony. Are you ready?" she asks, leaning forward to pull the hood up on my cloak, adjusting it so it covers my eyes from sight.

"As ready as I'll ever be," I say, pulling back a bit of the wrap dress to reveal a thigh belt with the dagger and a few potions tucked inside.

She begins to pour the yellow liquid in a circle around us, corking it and taking my hand.

"Remember your dream. She throws death magic at you. Please, for the love of the fates, dodge it," she says sternly. The yellow circle starts to glow and spin, rising through the air, creating a column of glowing golden light. I shut my eyes as the light begins to blind me and when I reopen them, I find myself outside of the castle, looking up at the high white walls.

"Quickly, join the crowd." Gran ushers me in, grasping my hand tightly. The line of people entering the castle walls all look ghostly; they're faces drawn in. They definitely don't look like they are about to attend a wedding. "Do you know how you are going to break the spell?"

"Well, shouting didn't work in the vision. I was going to try and send a message. Hopefully, I can find a bit of them still there and bring them forward." Gran looks at me sceptically. "It's the only shot we have!" I exclaim through a whisper, trying not to draw attention to us. We pass through the main doors of the castle and the crowd veers to the left to take their seats in the ballroom.

I stop still when the scene opens up in front of me. The white petals falling from the sky like snowflakes. The room filled with white flowers, some flowers I recognise, lilies and roses and others I don't, I presume they are native to the Fae world. I hug Gran, one last time, before I go ahead to find Hali. I find her exactly where she was in the dream. I wave my hand in front if her face, but I'm met with a blank stare, gazing straight through me as if I were a ghost. The thought sends a chill up my spine. I take her hands and call to her in her mind. *Hali, please snap out of it! It's me!* When her only response is a slow blink, I try to read her mind. Her mind sees her surroundings, but she has no feelings. She can't see me. She can't hear me.

"Please Hali!" I shout shaking her. Nothing. I turn and see Finn approaching the altar. I run to him, cupping his cheeks in my hands. *Please Finn, wake up.* His vacant eyes, burrowing into me. A burning tear streaks my face as the procession music starts, the petals begin turning black. The bride enters, her black dress, rippling along the floor like hot tar, the smell so putrid, the flowers begin to wilt in her presence. Her black veil covering her face. I pull back the hood of my cloak and take step towards the aisle.

"They're mine now," she says right on cue.

"What have you done to them?" I shout, my Gran standing in the back of the ballroom watching the events unfold, slowly making her way around the edge of the room.

"Me? I've done nothing." She says placing a hand on her heart. "They are all dreaming." My eyes widen in shock and she lets out a full bellied laugh. "What did you think I needed your father for? Very skilled that man, a little flick of the wrist and I can make dear daddy do whatever I wish," she says, goading.

"Why?"

"Because! I deserve the best, I deserve to rule over all. The Seelie have looked down on us for millennia! We were always the lower species! Never-ending wars, we lived in squalor, while they lived the high life! Well it's time for a new reign. Mine!" she says, pulling back her veil, revealing her face.

"Rose? You can't be serious!" I say, almost disappointed. Her face reddens with anger.

"I think it's time for you to go. Goodbye Thea." She throws her hand out, releasing the putrid smelling magic. I dive out of the way, pulling a dagger from my belt and throwing it at her, hitting her in the thigh. "Urrgh, you bitch!" she says and throw her hand one more time, throwing me through the tall glass windows and out into the courtyard. I scream, flying through the air until I hit the ground. Darkness enveloping me.

Chapter 17

I blink open my eyes, rubbing the haze from them. What the hell happened? My ears ringing, I feel the soft wet grass underneath me and move to sit up, finding one of my arms hanging limply at my side. Just like my dream. I reach into the ether for the potions sack, but before I can reach inside the brown scratchy material, the ballroom erupts in flames. Purple flames. I need to change the course of the dream. I throw the satchel over my shoulder and start to make my way back, dodging the Fae running towards me. Panicked and scattered, the people run for their lives, screaming. I push the best that I can, but the mob is reluctant to let me through knocking me to the ground. People are stepping on me. I try to get back up but I am pushed back harder, into the wet ground by the herd. I cradle my bad arm, trying to protect it from the thundering feet of the deranged guests. This is exactly why my mother never let me go to any concert with a mosh pit. I curl into a ball and try to protect myself, waiting for the mass to stop, until two strong hands scoop me off the ground and within a blink we're away from the castle and under a colossal tree, reaching up into the sky, on the outside of the castle walls. I look back to see the flames flickering and devouring all in its path, the flames turning violet with bursts of heat. I make a move to run back, but a firm hand grips my arm. Turning me towards them, I wince at the tenderness before looking at my captor.

"Finn!" I cry, wrapping my good arm around his neck. He hugs me tightly back.

"I'm so sorry. I didn't know what was going on. Your arm. Are you okay?" he asks, gently moving my wrist, to which I wince again. I feel for my bag, but it's gone. I must have dropped it in the crowd.

"I'll be fine. What happened? I got knocked out."

"I know, we heard you. We all heard you scream, and it woke us up. It shattered the dream we were all stuck in," he says, pulling me tightly too him again. "I heard you, I could you hear you calling to me, but I couldn't do anything, I'm so sorry," he says kissing my head.

"It's okay it wasn't your fault, but we need to get in there and make sure everyone is safe."

"No, stay here, you're hurt. I'll go."

"Not alone, Finn. We stick together." I kiss him hard, before running back to the castle. When he catches up, he grabs my hand and transports us back to the courtyard, most of the guests have made it out and are making their way out of the castle walls, through the purple smoke, billowing from the broken windows. I spot Gran tending to someone's ankle. Our eyes meet and she runs up to me and hugs me tightly.

"I thought I'd lost you," she whispers. I pull away quickly.

"We need to make sure everyone is out. Have you seen the fates, Hali or Rowan?" she gives me a sober look.

"The fates are safe; they have been transported to a safe house. But Rowan can't find Hali." I move to run back into the ballroom. Fire is licking the walls and crackling with the ingestion of the castle. "No! We need to make a plan. We can't run in there blind! If Brighid's still there, she has the upper hand, " Finn shouts.

"We can't just leave her in there. What if she's hurt or trapped?" I stand on my tip toes, looking over the crowd for her bright blonde hair. Rowan catches my eye and makes his way towards us.

Gran gives me a look. "You can find her. Use your head!" my Grandmother shouts tapping me on the temple. I let out an awkward giggle before concentrating.

I close my eyes focusing on her.

"Brighid is taking her to the mirror. If you can transport us to the Seer's tower, we can beat them there. The fire hasn't reached the west side of the castle."

"Althea, get the guards to start putting out this fire. Gather every Water Fae in attendance to start dousing it."

Rowan and I take Finn's hand and with a zip, we are in the Seer's tower. I move to step away as Finn crumples to the floor beside me, a dagger protruding out of his back.

"No!" I drop to my knees, putting pressure on the blood oozing wound. Three cloaked figures move into view behind us.

"Rowan Please, get him out of here," I cry. Rowan hooks Finn's arm over he his shoulder and heaves him off the floor.

"No, we can't leave you."

"I need to save Hali. Go!"

"Well, look who joined the party!" Brighid arrived, another cloaked figure dragging a bound Hali, beside her. "I'm glad you stuck around, Thea. I have a proposal for you." She gives an evil smile; her henchmen surround us.

"Please just let us go, you lost, you can't marry Finn."

"Marry Finn? Oh, you fool! Finn was a means to an end! I was going to kill him as soon as I was Queen anyway! So how about we cut to the chase. I will let everyone go if you come with me. You will do as I say and come willingly, or I will kill everyone here." She nods to the cloaked men, who step up behind Finn and Rowan, holding blades digging into their necks.

"No, please, Thea, you can't go with her," Finn pleads, his voice hoarse.

"You will let them all go?"

"Thea! No!" Hali shouts, struggling against her bindings.

"Yes, I will not harm them. For now." I look back at Finn, his eyes imploring me to listen to him. I kneel down and kiss him.

"Please," he begs, his complexion pasty.

"I'll go. Rowan, please get him to my grandmother."
"No!" Finn tries to fight. "Please, we can fix this together." I stroke the damp hairs from his forehead. Sweat slicks his skin.

"There's no time left. I choose for you to live." I kiss him again. "I love you."

"You can't say that and then leave with her!"

I turn to Rowan. "Take him now." My voice is barely audible, but he nods, and grips Finn tighter, moving towards the door.

I turn to Brighid. "Cut Hali free, once I see them leave, I will go with you." She nods to her henchman. I hug Hali tightly. "Please look after them. I'll escape as soon as I get the chance," I whisper, before she's is pushed towards the door.

"We can't have you seeing where we are taking you."

"No!" Finn shouts, before I feel a sharp pain in the back of my head and I black out.

Chapter 18

"Welcome, Thea, to your new home!" Brighid says mockingly, as I'm tossed like a bag of potatoes against a wall. I groggily try to sit up, placing my hands against my throbbing skull that feels like it's about to explode. "Just a little heads up for you. This room is charmed. You won't be able to use your stupid mind magic in here. You can't push your magic past these walls, if you do you won't like what happens. How did your father describe it again?" She places a finger against her chin in thought. "Oh! That's it. Mind melting. He couldn't form a sentence for days afterwards." She chuckled.

"What do you want with me? Hasn't your plan already failed?"

"Lesson one. There is always a plan B and it's usually a lot more destructive than plan A," she sneers, "and what do I want with you? Well you see, your dear old dad is getting a little... unreliable. I have seen what your powers can do. You are already much stronger than him, even if you are a half-breed. You are going to do exactly what I say, otherwise, I'll kill your father and make you watch. If you still don't behave, I will kill one friend at a time. One by one, finishing with your beloved Prince. They said you were fated. Didn't seem that way when you left him without a second thought." She laughs maniacally. "Hmm. I wonder if he survived? That was a pretty bad wound. For all you know he could already be dead! Would save me the hassle of killing him later." She laughs again, holding her stomach as if it was the funniest thing she had ever heard.

I pale at the thought. Surely, I would somehow know if he were dead? If we are fated, I would feel it or something right? What if these walls prevent me from feeling the link? He could be dead and I would be none-the-wiser.

"I can see you're worried, so I'll just leave you here for a while to think it over. Try anything and, well, you already know the consequences," she says, strutting from the room, like she's won. The door slams shut behind her, the sound of a bolt sliding into place. Bitch.

I look around the small round room. A tower maybe? No windows, only one door. I don't even know what land we are in. The floor is cold stone, completely bare. No bed, nothing. A cold draft, seeps under the door making me shiver. Maybe I should have thought and packed clothes in the ether. Not that I can access it anyway. I tug my cape around me, seeking warmth. This is my home for the foreseeable future.

My thoughts slip back to Finn, the panic in my chest overwhelms me. What if he didn't survive? He looked so weak.

I curl up in a ball. There isn't much else to do in here.

Chapter 19

Finn

"No!" I shout. Or try to, I suppose. My eyes feel so heavy, but I need to stay awake. They just knocked Thea out and are dragging her through the mirror. Dragging her, like she's a sack of bloody potatoes.

"You're going to regret this, Brighid," I growl, as she laughs, stepping through the mirror.

"I doubt that." She grins and then she's gone. Thea is gone.

Rowan is practically carrying me through the castle as my legs move tiredly, trying to keep pace. Hali has run ahead to find Althea, but I don't think I can stay awake much longer. I need to stay alive to save her, to bring her home.
She gave up everything to save me. Save me? Isn't it supposed to be the other way around? That's when I realised. She had told me she loved me and I didn't say it back.

"Stay with me, Finn. She will never forgive us if you die." I let out a dry laugh. "Hang on for her, pal."

We get to the courtyard, through the east exit of the castle, moving around the castle to where everyone is getting the help they need. I feel my eyes close for a minute before Hali slaps me hard across the face.

"You idiot! You can't die now. If you die, she dies!" I look at her with a confused look. Or what I think is one. I feel a little dizzy.

"What?" Rowan asks, just as confused as I am.

"I swear to god you men are so, clueless. You're fated! That's why it was so easy to find her, why you can feel her pain. That's why you dreamt about each other before ever meeting. I swear, you really needed me to spell that out for you?" she asks, shaking me a little, which didn't really help my dizziness. There is a pregnant pause where I assume myself and Rowan are staring at her agape. Then it all clicks into place.

"Oh shit." Rowan says, dumbfounded. Oh, shit, is definitely right pal. I imagine her now, alone and scared and there is nothing I can do to help her. Her beautiful big brown eyes scared and alone. Her face is the one I see when everything goes dark.

The end.

Author's Note

Thank you for reading 'A life beyond the mirror'.
I hope you enjoyed it as much as I enjoyed writing it! Please feel free to leave a review on Amazon and let me know what you think.

Please follow me on Amazon to find out when the next book in the series is released or join the facebook group at: Nicole Adams Reader's Group.

Printed in Poland
by Amazon Fulfillment
Poland Sp. z o.o., Wrocław